Cowboy & Tribe

SHANE FILER

ISBN: 978-9-5908-0017-7 (Paperback)
978-8-2461-1331-9 (eBook)

Published by Story Republik Press,
Wanganui,
New Zealand

For permissions:
contact@shanefiler.com
www.shanefiler.com

Dedicated, with love to Alena

LET'S SWAP:

YOUR EMAIL FOR FREE STUFF

Sign up for Shane Filer's no-spam newsletter and get news, updates and exclusive new material.

Details at the end of this book.

1

THE DROWNED

A lonely shore; she stands looking at waves, wondering where he has gone. Morning sun cuts a shimmering path over the Königssee's aqua-blue-green surface, and for a moment Saga Zimmer is blinded by bright violent light.

Sunlight takes just over eight minutes to reach the Earth. Saga remembers Michael explaining this to her as a child. If the Sun mysteriously and instantaneously disappeared, we on Earth wouldn't know it was gone until just over eight minutes after it happened. Only then, we would be plunged forever into darkness. Michael likes facts.

These are facts: Michael is four years older than Saga. He was close to their mother. He dislikes their father. Their mother died when Saga was twelve. Two years after Michael left home. Now Saga is twenty-one. She always looks up to Michael, and yesterday receives a letter from him.

The letter seems strange, a little disjointed and out of character. He writes of their trip to Italy last summer, but without his usual depth or color. She wonders if there's something wrong, yet how can there be? Michael's the most successful, extroverted, happy member of their family. Without

Michael, where would she be? Love is not a feeling she bandies around. Is it love she feels for her brother? She thinks about it and supposes so. These are not facts.

These are echoes.

Everyone's afraid the winter their mother lies dying of cancer in the upstairs bedroom, the house washed in a bleak tide of silence. They tiptoe around, sock feet over creaking floorboards, as she slips from being their mother to a small aged being clinging desperately to life. Why cling?

A television plays a *Loriot* movie and Michael and Saga are laughing. In the hall, the doctor and their father tread down the winding staircase. The front door breathes and exhales. After a few moments she registers their father standing in the doorway of the dark room, a flickering kaleidoscope projected across his blank face.

"How's mum?" Michael asks without looking up from the television.

Silence for a moment, then their father erupts, wrenching Michael violently from his chair by the shirt, shaking him like a dog with a toy. "How is your mother? She's dying. That's how she is—while you kids sit here laughing at *Loriot.* She is dying. Two weeks." Releasing Michael, he strides away to the dining room sinking into the cocoon of a Schnittke symphony. It's not spoken of again.

Days pass. Entering the kitchen in striped slippers, Saga begins preparing the evening meal. When her father comes home from work, she tells him dinner will be ready soon. He nods and makes his way upstairs. Saga listens as the door opens. It's silent for a long time and her father doesn't come downstairs. The potatoes have begun to boil on the stove. Dinner will be ruined.

Echoes.

Michael calls her from Vienna and asks her if she would like to take a trip to Italy in the summer. She says yes. That would be good.

Echoes.

At breakfast her father notices the letter from Michael on the table. He motions vaguely to it and asks how her brother is? Saga tells him to read it, but her father shrugs, returning to his newspaper. His new girlfriend is coming over later. They will eat alone in the dining room, a dark cathedral filled with distant concertos. Michael's good, she explains. He's doing well. Everything's fine.

Echoes.

The autumn leaves are turning rust-brown at the lake. Soon the trees will be stripped naked. Why did she come here? Saga remembers warm summers warmly. There are many tourists here today and she feels comforted. She wants water on her feet again, to be in water, to be close to water, yet she knows this time of year, the crystal streams flowing down from the Alps are freezing.

Ice-coldness. Her feet are in the water. Knee deep, startling cold, knife-bone splinters. The sheer sweep of the rocky cliffs rises before her and the dark, unfathomable deep stretches out ahead. A face ripples back at her, long dark chocolate-brown hair, green eyes, flawless lips and high cheekbones; a perfect mixture of her father's Teutonic and her mother's Swedish heritage.

Water lapping, her dress is wet, a jellyfish dancing macabre with the tide. People are staring. A man calls out to her from the shore, and she turns, but the sun is in her eyes, and she can't make out who he is.

"I am okay," she explains. "Don't worry. Everything is fine."

It's raining in the Austrian Alps when the train stops and Michael steps aboard. Saga smiles as he embraces her. "I've missed you," he speaks softly. He seems shorter to her or she seems taller. Saga moves a hand to his back and skims his jacket. On the train Michael begins to drink. Is it still a problem? Annoyed she stops talking.

Several hours wait in Verona; Saga and Michael brave the pin-cushion umbrella crowded streets and squares of sleety rain to visit the Museo Civico di Castelvecchio. Heels clicking on polished floors, she strides ahead of him through empty rooms.

Windows of the past line the bleached walls, beautiful oil time capsules of immortality. To him this is all death, to her it's life. The room is suddenly empty. Alone, she feels a sense of panic that she has lost Michael. It's only a momentary stab of fear, yet it's pervasive, and she feels transfixed by a wave of sharp heat through her body. Was he angry at her reaction to his drinking? Did he get bored with being dragged to one of these places again? Rushing through the maze of rooms, she's both relieved and upset to find him chatting up a tourist under the watchful eye of Bellini's *Madonna with Child.* A barefoot, tanned girl with an Antipodean accent; Saga hurries her along with an icy white stare.

In the train to the coast Michael is back to his old self, telling her of the beauty of physics and his work on quantum theory; fractal dimensions and Mandelbrot's mathematical simplicity fly above her head. As a teenager he dreamed of being a physicist. Saga dreamed merely of new outfits. Dreams come true.

Michael asks if she has anyone new in her life, and Saga replies quickly no. There are people who come and go, but there is no one.

"You never wanted to be in love?" he asks sipping his beer.

Given up chastising her older brother, she too drinks chilled white wine, and a more relaxed, more honest mood flows.

"No, I'm not capable of it." The silence she leaves compels her to fill it. "I don't like being touched. I dislike the pretense of emotional intimacy."

"Why don't you work? Or at least finish your degree?"

"I'm too beautiful to work," her lips delicately curve at the edges.

"Get out of that house and stop relying on Dad giving you money. He changed after Mum died. It engulfed him and he was never the same. I saw him as a weak individual and I wanted to be strong like our mother."

"I know. Did you know he beat me up once?" Saga asks. "Not long after you'd left, I'd been out with a boy till late. He attacked me and hit me when I returned home. He didn't say anything, and I didn't say anything. I can't be mad at him forever. Why should I? If I hate him for everything he did to us I would be miserable. There are other ways I can hurt myself."

The train arrives at Vernazza as the last of the beer laps against sheer polished walls in Michael's glass.

The next morning Saga waits in the hotel lobby while Michael, having forgotten his wallet, returns to their room. Doors open and shut at the entrance, movement and voices; it's the accent which makes her look up first, the dropped vowels of the barefoot girl from Verona. Walking to the reception desk, the girl struggles to remove a large grey hiking pack from her back. Has she followed them here? Did Michael tell her to come? But no—the door opens again and there's another man behind her. He touches her lower back. So she found someone after all. The girl glances in Saga's direction but fails to recognize her. In that second, the man stares at Saga and his eyes cut right through her. He's blond, dressed well in casual jeans and a white jacket, perhaps of subtle Western European origin… French… Dutch…? Saga feels an instant of vulnerability. His eyes follow her long legs and she turns to flee, but Michael is suddenly behind her and she is momentarily glad. Yet Michael smells of alcohol. When they return, she will check the mini-bar.

Michael hires a small boat and they row out to a secluded island, more rock. It's a startling contrast to the pancake-stacked tourist beaches.

"Ah solitude," Michael remarks and dives into the sea.

Saga sits on a rock, her feet circling in the warm Mediterranean. "It's so quiet—it seems sad. I'm used to people around."

"It's the water that's sad, listen to the sound."

A gentle harmonic wash. She listens and realizes he's right. The ocean sounds sad. Letting herself slip from the rock into the deep water, she soon goes under. When she surfaces, Michael is a boy again beside her, head bobbing in the icy blue of a Bavarian Lake. Their mother is there, watching protectively from the shore. Sun reflects across water and she closes her eyes.

When Saga opens her eyes, everything is quiet; the steady slow lap of the waves on shore bring her from that world, into this one. Skin covered in sand, she sits up. Sunburned; did she fall asleep? A lonely shore; she stands looking at waves, wondering where he has gone. A voice calls, calling his name steadily. Soon she will be screaming but no sound comes back. The boat is empty.

The world ends, gasping onward.

Rowing back to shore is long and painful. Her hands are blistered. When did the sunburn stop hurting? Saga returns and pays for the boat, then makes her way back to the hotel. Upstairs the room's empty, and so too is the mini-bar. She showers. Things. She must do things. She rubs moisturizer on her burned skin, covers her palms in intricate Band-Aid patterns, changes into fresh clothes and makes her way downstairs.

The bar is near empty. Only the Dutchman. What is that accent? She is trying to make it out. Oh, she was wrong—it's Swedish. His girlfriend in bare feet is nowhere to be seen. Perhaps she went to buy shoes? A tiny smile forms. The newly identified Swede passes her a glance, supposing it was for him. Saga turns away and orders a drink. Then another.

Sometime later he's groping her on the floor of her bedroom. There's a loud television screaming. She wishes she could switch the channel. He's taking off her clothes, but she docsn't scc him and he doesn't see her.

Shopping bags straddle cafe table legs in Augsburg's Rathausplatz; Saga and her friends slip into their chairs and order food and wine. They are among her oldest school friends and the first thing they want to know about is Italy. She shows them a photo—it's of Michael at a cafe in Verona, and they immediately want to know about Michael?

"Michael's fine," she tells them. "But he has gone away for a while. It's his work. It's taken him to the Antipodes."

Michael is doing so amazingly well for himself. He is the successful, together one. Michael will always be a success. She will always look up to him. Sometimes she knows she will miss him, but she has always missed him, since he left home and left her alone.

What does it mean anyway—to have someone you care about in your life? Isn't it just a bit dangerous? Aren't you really just asking for trouble? What happens if they decide to suddenly go away, to drift away to the Antipodes? Where does that leave you? No, she's happier the way she is. Her father gives her money to buy things. Anything she asks for. Earlier she made the decision to move to the flat her father owns in Munich. Michael would be proud. Of course, he will have to repaint and refurnish it first. Just the last month she began seeing a man regularly. A lawyer from her father's firm, he takes her out to dinner often. He brought her the most expensive silver necklace, and she wears it almost every day. He talks to her about things she has no interest in, and she knows she talks about nothing to him, yet she is beginning to imagine married life with him. Life is changing for her, and it is getting better.

Michael's happy for her too. He told her so in his letters from far away. Vaguely it troubles her that he doesn't quite sound himself, but perhaps it's just that he's missing Europe. His handwriting too—it has always been a little like her own. It's a fact she keeps reminding herself of. It's like Michael would say. Her future stretches promisingly ahead. Everything is good. It's really going to be fine. She will be fine too.

On tourist boats on the Königssee the tour guides play a shiny brass instrument called a flugelhorn—which can echo back from the sheet rock walls up to seven times. Saga Zimmer listens now to its first sounding, and waits for subsequent echoes.

2

THE SECRET WORLD OF ABBY NORMAL

Once only milk was homogenized.

This is a story about a world not unlike your own. A grey world where all art has become as vanilla as Taylor Swift, mass marketed music, film, art, that you can buy at the nearest Starbucks with sprinkles on top. I'm sure somewhere out there in the world... some sincere, caring, intelligent person is crying, because all they want is something real, something true. Just something unique that only their culture can give them or teach them. They won't find it here, I don't think. Here, all book and music stores are the same store selling the same product. Television, film and other media limit diversity to numb minds and ensure consistent profits.

Screw it, dumb fucks. Who am I kidding? It's your world.

It's also the story of Abby Normal.

No one knew quite where Abby came from or indeed how she came to be—vomited from the global tides of grey? Unlikely. The global tides of grey actually didn't know very much, and that was the way they liked it. That was the way the

Corporation liked it too. What everyone liked was the masses went about their lives, productively minding their own business, working long hours, recreation time spent drenched in triviality. They were happy. Told many lies, they asked no questions, content as the Corporation shit into their mouth, mind and body and told them to like it.

Then Abby appeared. The first signs that all was not normal, that all would never be normal again, appeared over several days as dashes of color; giant canvas paintings nailed on grey urban walls, and enigmatic slogans like: *Feel, Fear or Fuck.* A little much, you may think perhaps? But please keep in mind Abby has set out with a very peculiar and difficult goal: to wake an *anesthetized* society.

Upon a skyline of hideously plaintive glass architecture, air-pods dip to and fro (yeah, we finally got flying cars. We must thank the Corporation for something. Credit where credit's due). High above the canopy of the city, a young woman displays an elfish grin as she pulls down her mask, adjusts the goggles and stares down at the carefully arranged dominoes. Time to flick some over.

Abby pushes the joystick forward, and banshee-screams into the wind as the air-pod plunges. She skims across a street purposely too low, dropping a few feet to shake windows of a music megastore, and sticks out her tongue at the startled staff and customers alike. A minor distraction.

Pulling back on the controls sends the air-pod into a steep climb. *Amelia Mary Earhart*, feminist symbol, aviator mentor, would be proud. Yet enough fun, there's work to be done. A statement to be made. Sliding back the Plexiglas canopy, Abby reaches across to a heavy sack on the passenger seat. Another pass at breakneck speed as she throws books to the streets below. *In Search of Lost Time* by Marcel Proust. *Don Quixote* by Miguel de Cervantes. *Ulysses* by James Joyce. *The* Great *Gatsby* by F. Scott Fitzgerald. *Moby Dick* by Herman Melville. *Hamlet* by William Shakespeare. *War and Peace* by Leo Tolstoy. *The Odyssey* by Homer.

It's raining literature…

Pedestrians scramble to dodge, side-step and snatch items in the sudden downpour. *Catch-22* by Joseph Heller slams into a delivery man sending parcels flying. An old woman pisses her pants upon picking up *To the Lighthouse* by Virginia Woolf. A businessman keels over, subjected to a glancing blow of *The Trial* by Franz Kafka.

Then as quickly as she arrived, Abby's away, surfing a passing updraft.

Take that normal people!

The Art Critic doesn't like it. Not at all.

"Too gauche," he decides.

"Too retro," his assistants echo, shaking heads like dismayed parrots, watching as he strides up and down—a caged and angry beast. "Who's responsible for this?"

No one knows.

The Art Critic has to know. It's his job after all. A tall and ambitious man, with an important job—he oversees all art disseminated into society by the Corporation.

Three hundred years ago there were no corporations, imagine that? The 20th century saw that number explode, but corporations eat themselves and just one remained standing, a brutal, glistening, apex predator.

The Art Critic—is a nickname (official role: CEO, Media Creation and Distribution)—an apt one, as after all it's his role to make (literally) artists. Truth be told, the Art Critic's passion is for leadership and management and while his route to media had been via the consumer electronics industry, it could have equally been through fast food or pet food. Within the oligarchy there are many diverse paths for horizontal or vertical career movement for the astute individual. The Art Critic is, if nothing else, very astute.

In the grand, modern reception of the Corporation, the Art Critic meets with police officers assigned to the case. His assistant, Miss Honeypop provides everyone with tea and coffee and hovers bee-like; her hair tied back, black-rimmed glasses propped on a thin nose, she's almost invisible—a grey mouse. But oh, if there's one lesson I've learned, it's to pay attention to the grey mice of this world.

"This is Inspector Fitch, and Detective Abercrombie," the mouse squeaks, then hippity-hops back to her desk. Don't worry we haven't seen the last of her, not by a long shot.

"We have a problem," the Art Critic says, leading the policemen towards a tall glass elevator.

"It's a serious business," the inspector agrees. "There hasn't been unsanctioned artistic activity in thirty years. We take a very dim view of it."

"You've never been here before, have you?" the Art Critic asks. "Let me give you a guided tour."

Exiting the elevator, they are apparitions on treadmills, sweeping past rooms where vast computers hum like drone bees and printing presses spit out product with clinical precision.

"Down here all art is created—books, paintings, comics and films. We call this computer system the Ghost. Earlier this century it became common for many big name writers to have their books scripted by ghost writers. Today we eliminate the human element entirely. Author brands are created and carefully positioned. Ghost writes the story. We just select the genre, some character options and the story is output, edited, typeset, and ready for instant printing, digital distribution and marketing. The movie adaption and merchandise are ready to go in hours."

The two policemen nod, impressed.

It becomes cooler further down into the basement where the artists toil. These artists do not need heat, nor do they require breaks, inspiration or air, for they are merely Ghost's algorithms slashing relentless images onto passive, brumal displays and canvas.

"Art is very dangerous. Few realize the power of art, the inner dreams it may awaken in each of us, the desire of thought, to reach beyond consciousness into the realms of the unknown. Conversely, it can also trigger mental inertia, the coma-like state brought on by being surrounded by the trivial, the weakly aesthetic, total meaningless and uninspiring."

On cue insipid music snakes through airwaves, uncoiling itself through speaker wires:

Heartbreakers gonna break, break, break, break, break,
And the fakers gonna fake, fake, fake, fake, fake

"Having our hands on the throat of all media and art we keep the people in a somnambulant state. We cannot have unauthorized art."

"Cannot have it," the inspector echoes. "Fear not, our best people are on it. Soon we'll have those responsible."

Here ends the tour.

Tap tap tap. The Art Critic sits alone with Ghost. I'll share a secret only I know: The Art Critic has a hobby. He wouldn't call it a hobby. A game. He likes to sit down here, hiding from the offices where people roam. He sits and wonders about the sacrifices he has made to get to the top; two divorces and ungrateful, hateful children. His game: he taps on the screen and gives Ghost ideas for the next big thing. *An executive finds it lonely at the top and embarks on an affair with his younger assistant.*

Miss Honeypop pops into his mind. No one notices her, yet he notices her.

Piped music changes, a different tempo now, swirling strings and violins enacting sadness… enticing… a tear. It's very bad, he realizes reaching for the nearest phone. It's subversive, even. The art-terrorist has hijacked the airways.

It's Bach.

"What do you mean you're doing all you can? Block the transmission!"

A voice begins to speak through music. A bright and chirpy female voice, ever so soothing. It's a voice that can only ever bring trouble.

"Hello dear listeners, I am bored, bored, bored, and when I get bored, I get cranky. I want to rock the boat. Do you ever feel like this? Hmmm, probably not I guess. Oh, we haven't been properly introduced. You can call me Abby Normal—that's my name. You may think it's not normal? It's the most normal name that I can think of. Here is something which isn't normal: art created and controlled by corporations. I don't like it, oh no. A free press is essential for a free society. It's true of art also. Through free art, real issues that affect our lives are reflected back. Yet both free speech and free art has been taken from us slowly over time by stupid people and greedy corporations, and we let it happen. It makes me sad, mad even. So I'm going to do something about it, just see if I don't —"

At last she's cut off.

Copies of *In the Boardroom* are reeling off the press with a soft rain-like pitter-patter. The Art Critic consoles himself in a world of fiction, sits and begins to read.

Well dear readers, you've heard from Abby and seen what she can do, what else would you like to know? What does Abby look like? Well the more astute of you will realize Abby is rather a grey mouse, and that's how she likes it. Almost no one ever looks at Abby or notices her. She could be anyone and that's just how Abby Normal likes it.

But she's not just anyone. A child drawing. A teenager writing poems. If not actively discouraged, she's not encouraged. Abigail is a young woman studying computer programming. Abigail Honeypop is a cog sitting behind a corporate desk. Wait—before you accuse her of selling out it has to be said that everyone works for the Corporation. Entrepreneurship requires creativity, and we sure stamped that out years ago. Now, if you're like Abby and born into the masses, although not one of the masses, your choices are few. You conform or you... well you conform really.

But how does our grey mouse cope with this day to day grind? Day-dreaming for a start. Plotting, planning. This is where the seeds are sown, but what caused the first creative sprout to raise its head from beneath this arid soil?

Perhaps it can be found, like most things, in her average day? In a world of ordinariness, Abby appears ordinary. She barely makes conversation with co-workers, and if she does, it's usually small talk, about the weather (yeah, it's nice), or the latest Vlad Velocity movie (yeah, he's hot).

Perhaps not.

A day ends, and Abby takes the train back to her apartment.

Perhaps something stirs here?

Inside the apartment a cat shuffles down the stairs to greet her. Abby picks him up, an old cat she has had since childhood. Yes, Abby's still relatively young. Riffling through the freezer, she removes a frozen packaged dinner. A dinner for one, for she is alone. Completely so.

And in that loneliness, she does something out of the ordinary. Abby, sits on a couch, a notepad and pen in hand, and begins to write. This is no shopping list. This is a story, a howling spirit inside her, screaming at the non-existence of her day.

I begin to think that I've become exactly like Yarrow from Ursula Le Guin's book—like a little fish in the water; defenseless but impossible to catch. I don't think anyone is going to catch me.

This is what she does every day. She writes, draws or paints. This immense desire to create simmers within her, before love and shelter; second only in necessity to nourishment. Millions exist without love, but few survive in a complete vacuum. Her stories, her drawings, her ideas, become friends, life, and in the absence of people, fill up rooms.

Mirror, Mirror on my wall. When you stand in front of me and look at me, what do you know of my grief and what do I know of yours?

Earlier: a small click, a grim sense of satisfaction, as Abby presses *send.* Abby could easily have destroyed Ghost, a lethal virus would have been just as easy for her to create and transmit, but where is the creativity in that? No, her virus did something quite different. (I have to thank her for that). The world we will wake into tomorrow will be a different one.

Earlier even: *An art critic falls in love with the artist whose work he must deride.* The Art Critic lifts the book and inhales the scent of fresh ink. He must know how this story ends: *The Secret World of Abby Normal.*

The day begins as any other, normal; changes imperceptible until electronic devices are activated. Suddenly, there's a change in the airwaves when people switch on their radios—gone are the banal prank DJs, and manufactured pop sensations. Televisions are silent black holes in living rooms. At first, the masses are confused—patting electronics like dying dogs, trying to coax them back to life. When they do vibrate and flicker, something people haven't expected is waiting. New movies, music, books, art exhibitions. At first, they're not sure what is different or what to make of it, but after a while they begin to watch, listen, read and… think.

"It's her—Abby Normal. She's done something. Sent a virus through our system!" The Art Critic arrives at work to find disaster. Police pour over data.

"We've analyzed it, and the virus contains within it the complete works of Shelley, Faulkner, Kerouac, Shakespeare, in fact all great literature from antiquity to the 20th Century; the films of David Lynch, Antonioni, Bergman, the French New Wave, Scorsese's seventies output and other selected works; the music of Gershwin, Tchaikovsky, a plethora of classical music, the Beatles, the Doors, Joy Division, punk and post-punk; art from the romantic period, to pop-art. It seems she has… well..." Inspector Fitch hesitates.

"Go on—speak up man!"

"She's educated the computer. She's inspired it. Ghost can no longer produce bad art—it's pumping out original classics by the score. We can't shut it off. No one can stop it."

"Can you trace where it came from?"

"That's the good news. We can and have, but you won't like it."

(No.)

"It came from here. Someone in the company."

The Art Critic stares for a moment into space, before his eye-line fixes on Miss Honeypop's empty desk. No one notices the grey mouse. Where is Miss Honeypop?

She didn't come in today.

Fetch me her personnel file. Does anyone know her first name?

Abigail knew that despite her best efforts they would trace the source of the virus back to her.

From: The Secret World of Abby Normal, 1st Edition, 2055, Corporate Press.

"Death to corporate art—you'll never take me alive!" Abby Normal opens fire with her paint-gun; Andy Warhol sunflowers pop into life across the chests of the police squad as they break down her door. Abby pulls on her mask, the slashed femininity, black, white and red of Picasso's The Dream, and makes her escape out the window via the fire escape.

On the fortieth level car-park her air-pod is waiting. Rushing forwards, she's momentarily swayed as real machine gun fire cuts across the pavement in front of her, a warning burst. Abby looks up to see the air-pod of the Art Critic dropping like a large, rotting, white egg towards her.

"Surrender, you can't escape!" he cries.

Abby coaxes her pod into the air, throwing books to the streets to gain height.

The sky is dotted with malevolent white stars all spiraling in her direction. He's right. She can't escape. Yet for Abby, escape back into the masses was never an appealing option. A series of bullets strafe her air-pod and smoke begins billowing from its engine. Out of control, it dips towards a rooftop and crashes in a heap of cables and satellite dishes.

The Art critic touches down nearby while his minions circle. Abby crawls to the roof edge, leaving behind bloody stripes on concrete. Slowly, she drags herself to her feet and turns.

Absorbed, still reading, the Art Critic begins to walk up the stairs. He has no idea how this will end, yet before he gets even close to the door, he smells gas, and then he knows.

It ends badly.

For a moment he expects her to say something. A final cry of defiance perhaps? Instead, he hears his own voice breaking the silence.

"Miss Honeypop, I know it's you. Take off your mask. I love you."

Hesitating for only a second, Abby obeys. Her hair has lost its mousy tincture in the bright sun, and glows almost red. Her eyes meet his, then flicker nervously to the ledge and the certain drop to death.

"Don't do it Miss Honeypop. I can fix this. I'm the Art Critic. I can publish your book. I can arrange showings for your paintings. It's not too late."

Abby's eyes soften, and she limps towards him with her arms outstretched. He feels sudden and real relief, and knows all will be okay, knows they will finally be happy together.

This is not how it ends. The Art Critic closes the book. It ends with Fitch describing to him how she sealed up the doors of the apartment very carefully, wrote a short note, a word on the wall, then turned on the gas and lay on the floor with her cat.

"Can I see?" the Art Critic asks. "I should identify her."

"It's not a pretty picture."

When you stand in front of me and look at me, what do you know of my grief and what do I know of yours?

He holds the note. The sheet falls. It's her. He stands back. The apartment looks lonely. She looks lonely on the floor. Is she everything we have feared? On the mirror above her, scrawled in pink lipstick: *Unsatisfied.*

There are meetings, there are debriefings and there are demotions in the aftermath. It will take months, perhaps years to have Ghost up and running again. The Corporation's focus groups suggest the public will not understand the real art forced upon them. They do not wish to think. They never did. And when has a focus group ever been wrong?

The Art Critic has a new office. Smaller. Of course, he's no longer the Art Critic. It's a long way down the corporate ladder. What is he now? What will the people do? Who knows, and it's no longer his concern. He doesn't know what his concern is really. No one's yet spelled out the job for him. It's certain to be something tedious though. For the first morning he wanders around his new office, setting up stationary, plants, familiarizing himself with the staff coffee machine. No one really talks to him in the new department. No one wants to be his friend. *Screw them,* he tells himself, but it hurts. Who doesn't want to be liked? Who wants to be lonely forever?

He returns alone to his office. It seems even starker than when he left it. A chair invites him to sit, and he does so. Laid out on the desk, a white sheet of paper. As a child, his favorite color was cobalt-blue, like the ocean. He holds a pen in his hand and moves it around the page. Doodling at first, but then the inky peregrinations take on greater purpose, slowly filling the page out with a memory.

He leaves it and walks around the room some more, slowly, cautiously returning to the desk and peers down.

It's not that good frankly. The shaky hand of a talented amateur. But we both have our pain, our loss, our inspiration and need to start somewhere.

That's just what I intend to do right now.

3

BLACK FAIRY

Raz-ee is her dancer name, and also the name of the small tattered Arabian doll she carries child-like through the night, sometimes slipped into the edges of her G-string. Much is lost in the dim past, but she still remembers where the doll came from. A child who collected stamps and dolls from faraway places with exotic names like *Umm al-Quwain*. At first, it was stunt, a glib point of difference from the other girls in the club, but as she looks into the face of the doll, hair covered neatly in a black hijab, she can't ever imagine being without Raz-ee. She's not sure if the spelling is right. Something's not right. Something bothers her a little, but as desirous eyes trail her descent with the slim silver pole between her legs, she soon discards the thought. The black fairy wings on her back flutter. Most people believe they are fake.

The cold London night air causes her pause as she exits the club. A group of women passes, one pausing to spit: "Stripper!"

Two steps across the road and the club door opens. A drunken patron approaches and a smile across the Louise Brooks-white china of her face. She steps with determination across the road, long black coat billowing behind.

"You want me? Come to me then."

The man's pottery clay, wet in her hands. He steps onto the road and is in an instant run down by a speeding truck. Footsteps scatter amid screams as she kneels with curiosity to touch blood in the gutter. She is the Black Fairy.

"There be three kindes of fairies, the black, the white, and the green, which black be the woorst."
– John Walsh (1566)

A woman in white approaches, an icy albino ghost in a sheet.

I have watched you for a long time. We have all watched you.

And what have you seen?

Pettiness. Selfishness. Sometimes a mild sense of mischief, and sometimes, like tonight, actions altogether more serious and deadly.

I am Black Fairy. It is my nature.

Why do you hate them so? Is it because you were once one of them?

My pettiness has to come from somewhere.

Something has to be done. An example. A lesson in humanity. I just took away your power, because only I can. You're human again.

Fuck.

They send me to the House of the Others.

Within this house there are no clocks. Time is meaningless. I feel like the newborn lamb being readied for the slaughter, yet it is a different kind of death that awaits me.

"Razieh, don't forget your coat, it's cold outside."

"Razieh, will you pass the salt please?"

Sometimes I forget who I was while we sit at the table and make polite dinner conversation. My new mother, father and brother tire me, so I cannot concentrate on their words or form sentences, and I become ghost-like in their presence. It infuriates them.

"I feel like a prisoner here," I explain. The salt cellar is black and the pepper cellar white. White suggests purity, and blackness evil. Every religion has its own concept of good and evil, right and wrong, black and white. The floor is black and the walls white. My mother wears black and my father white. White is the color of milk and fresh snow. Black is the color of my true love's hair.

"Nothing is ever black and white," she tells me as if she believes it.

Within the black and white world of the House of the Others I begin to plan my escape. Difficult because I must guard my thoughts for the White Fairy is lingering at the edge of reality. I am watched.

There are physical walls and there are mental walls. For even if I were to escape, who would help me? Everyone is on the side of the White Fairy. I know I am evil. These things I do, because I do.

Escape takes quite a lot of planning. With my powers the White Fairy took my wings. It's not like I can fly away. Once I know that I am going, I spend a few days casing the layout of the yard. I know I must escape by darkness. The others will not let me leave the house alone. They take me with them everywhere. At night the yard is a spider-web of infra-red signals, encased in a tall concrete wall. Near the western side of the building there is a tree hanging over from the street. Over the course of the week I nudge a large compost bin towards it, a few inches at a time, so the movement to the casual observer is imperceptible.

Then the time comes and I tie the white bed sheets together, dropping through my window into the night. I stay close to the building, under the trajectory of the motion sensors. Quickly I climb the bin, scale the tree, then down the other side, and I am free from the House of the Others.

But what kind of freedom is it, when I am condemned to the shadows? I live in isolation, in a world of darkness. What I need is my powers back, but the only one who can give them back is the White Fairy, and who am I to stand against her?

For a while I content myself to hide in among the blank faced black sheets. When I need to support myself I lose myself dancing in dark clubs; Manchester's twin gems of the Smith's *How Soon is Now?* and Joy Division's *Love Will Tear Us Apart* become my signatures while the men stare up unknowingly at my swirling star turn.

Freedom is fleeting. The White Fairy tracks me down herself, or I am betrayed. I am awoken to a bone-white flash of movement across a small black room. I leap back in the bed in white-fear, while she casually pulls up a chair across from me, her teeth shining a pearl smile.

"Why do you not do as I ask?" she hisses.

"I am Black Fairy. I live free as I desire, not trapped in a prison of living as Others wish me to. I do not need your concern or your smothering desire. You can take my power, but you can never change me. Never, ever. I am Black Fairy."

Red. Red. Red. I begin to laugh as I see her white sheer satin dress stained crimson. That is moments before I realize it's my blood. Her skin is under my fingernails, but those are only defensive wounds. Once I could have torn her apart and I would have if I had to. But not now. White Fairy is far stronger. She beats me with cold precision; a skilled surgeon she knows where to place each blow to cause maximum pain, skin tears and blood vessels burst in violet-blue. She does enough not to break any bones. All I see is her death-bride red-splattered face slashed into a maniac grin. It's over in seconds.

"So," she stands and asks, "Don't you think it's time you went home?"

I am trying to hold on to reality, but it's a shifting unpleasant thing, out of reach of my blood-fingers. Two trails on the floor-boards. Blood leads in different directions, but which one to follow? Taking my arm, the White Fairy drags me one way towards the door, but this is not the way I want to go. The other pool of blood rivers to a doll sitting in a corner. The door closes. I close.

Within the mirror the image of Razieh adjusts the black hijab. For it is an image—not really her. The real her rests in hands. Impassively the face that stares back is exotic; peaked eyebrows and black eyes, carved in the snow of too much powder on dark skin. She applies red to the mix, at first tracing the outline of her lips, then the lines become too much to stick to, too much coloring between lines, and the lipstick smears across her face. Yes, it looks good. Razieh smiles in a death-clown-grin.

The day wakes, sun upon always blue sky; outside morning prayer has begun. She walks across the floor. She is fifteen but who would know? Her husband of two years lies prone on the bed. He wears his favorite white thawb, perfect but for the rosette stain at his breast. The bloody razor knife lies discarded on the floor.

Razieh looks to the open door. The maid has been and gone while she was in the bathroom. Somewhere in the world that lies beyond there are sirens. She walks to the window and sees flashing lights. Someone did something wrong, and someone will be punished. It's black and white. But not her. In her hands she holds the Black Fairy doll. The very favorite in her collection. She is Razieh, the Black Fairy.

There's freedom beyond the window. Across the city, people wake to a life. An unfurling flutter. Upon her back, her wings have returned, shimmering, translucent ebony. Razieh, the Black Fairy stands on the ledge, surveying the world below. She takes one further step. This is her freedom.

The echo of wings.

4

KUNDERAESQUE

It's only after I realize that Milan Kundera, the famed Czech writer was born not far from where I'm staying, that I start to wonder what it would be to live within a Kundera novel? To feel the same existential pathos as his characters? To engage in isolated moments of steamy, but ultimately meaningless sex? To feel the persecution of a bleak and detached totalitarian regime. I also wonder why there is the word Kafkaesque, but not Kunderaesque?

Milan Kundera left Czechoslovakia after the 1968 Prague Spring, when he was fired from his teaching job and his books banned. He has lived in France since 1975 and is reputed to rarely visit his homeland. The Czech Republic has yet to create a museum for Milan Kundera despite his position as the most celebrated Czech writer of his generation. A love/hate relationship perhaps perpetrated by Kundera's own insistence that his works should be filed under *French* Literature.

Into the eighties. Kundera was a towering wunderkind of art-lit. *The Unbearable Lightness of Being* had been released in France in 1984. If you wanted to sleep with deep serious university girls, then you had to have the right answer to the inevitable question: "Do you like Milan Kundera?"

The Kundera light has faded a little. Now in his nineties he still continues to write, his most recent novel being *The Festival of Insignificance* published in 2015.

I ponder Kundera as I walk past Purkyňova 6, and decide that I will go ask whoever lives there if I can see the place Kundera grew up. Of course, I don't speak Czech and neither does the crone who comes to the door speak English. She either assumes I am there to sell or steal something, and slams the door shut quick. I am no closer to learning anything new about Kundera.

Then I hit upon an idea. I will spend a day living life as if I am in one of the master's novels. I will only do things or say things that his characters did or said. I will discover what it's like to live in a Kunderaesque way. Just for one day.

To prepare I rummage through Czech vintage clothing stores. My aim is to find some authentic menswear from the communist era that Milan Kundera might have actually worn. I find a plain white shirt with a narrow collar that to me says Marx all over. The label reads: *Made in Bangladesh.* There's a great mixed-tweed blazer with leather patch elbows. *Made in China.* No matter. I finish the outfit off with some beige polyester flare pants and simple black Oxford shoes. They turn out, disappointingly, to be *Clarks.*

The day of Kunderaesque has arrived. Observing over my shoulder, in the mirror, my girlfriend (A.) tells me I look like a seventies university lecturer, (ah-ha this is just the look I'm going for)—alternatively a seventies porn star. Damn.

I begin in Brno's Freedom Square, lamenting to a stranger on a bench the ugliness engraved upon its face as Ludvik did in The Joke. "So here I am," I tell him. "Home again after all those years. Here in the main square I that I feel no emotion for whatsoever."

"I like the penis clock," he says and snaps a photo. Turns out he's an American tourist. The amusing spectacle of the penis clock was absent in Milan Kundera's day. I wonder if it had existed back then, would his books have been more cheerful?

Talk a friend into pretending to be a hitchhiker, so I can pick her up and pretend not to know each other like the unnamed characters in *Laughable Loves.* Stop at gas station like they do, and she walks on ahead. Fill up car, then exit onto motorway. Realize I took the wrong off-ramp and have to loop around for twenty minutes to find my way back. She's broken a heel and is sitting, grumpily on the grass. "Where are you headed, miss?" I ask. "Are you going to Bystrica?"

"I just want to go home," she replies.

Make it to dive-bar mid-morning. Order a Starobrno beer, like the kind Milan Kundera probably drank. Turn to random drunk beside me and ask: "Isn't it nonsensical for me to get up in the morning? To go to work? To strive for anything? To belong to a nation just because I was born that way?" Just as Milan Kundera said once in an interview. Drunk shrugs and supposes so.

Go to post office to collect a parcel. Wait for eternity in the bland surroundings of the Czech public service. Finally, stand in front of austere glass counter while an unsmiling worker scrutinizes my ID. Begin to understand a little of how

Kundera must have felt when he was dragged in for questioning over his subversive writings in former Czechoslovakia. Woman hands out a paper which I sign under duress. She hands me my parcel in a Kunderaesque way.

Get talking to attractive Czech girl on tram. Ask her if she will come back to my apartment and strip for me, like Tomas commands of women in *The Unbearable Lightness of Being.* She politely declines. As she leaves tram, I notice she is dressed Czech style with ugly pattern leggings and brightly colored miss-matched top. Realize that this is likely the reason Czech women are often ordered to strip in Kundera's novels. He hated their outfits.

Buy bowler hat and take it home to girlfriend. Ask A. if she will wear it while I take photos of her kneeling on the floor on a mirror like Sabina asks of Tereza in the film of *The Unbearable Lightness of Being.* "Nude photos?" she asks. "Yes," I reply. She agrees.

After tell her that our female dog likes her more which means the dog's a lesbian (just like Tomas tells Tereza in *The Unbearable Lightness of Being*). She points out we don't have a dog, only a cat who's a boy and asks if this makes him straight?

Visit mall where clothing store is loudly playing K-pop. When young shop assistant asks me if I want any help, I reply: "In the past people would listen to music out of love for music, nowadays it roars everywhere and all the time, so that we can't tell beginning from end; sewage-water music in which music is dying." Just as Kundera writes in *Ignorance.* Guessing I'm not going to buy anything, shop assistant walks away.

Evening falls. End day of Kunderaesque by meeting A. at a cemetery. A woman tending a grave politely nods good evening to us and I tell her I very much long for Czech cemeteries, like Sabina does in *The Unbearable Lightness of Being*. Confused, she asks why. I stammer something about the French not burying the bones deep enough.

"So how was your day?" A. asks. "Was it all you hoped?"

It was enlightening I have to admit. I really do now assume the men demanding women take off their clothes in Kundera novels is only partly due to the attractiveness of Czech women, but mostly due to the unattractiveness of their clothes. There was a practicality I hadn't quite appreciated in his novels until today.

It's certainly not easy living your life like a Kundera character though. Normal people stare at you strangely when you wax philosophically about the human condition. You begin to feel persecuted by the greyness of the system. You begin to feel every person you encounter is fictional. You begin to feel you're even fictional. German is the definitive philosophical language as far as Kundera is concerned too, so you really need to read a lot of Nietzsche. A bowler hat is also essential to truly experience a Kunderaesque world. It's a mysterious world. A bold world. A better world. I still wonder why there is no word for it.

"Kunderovsky," A. says. "We Czechs have a word for it."

5

I'M WITH STUPID

"*Two things are infinite: the universe and human stupidity; and I'm not sure about the universe.* So said Albert Einstein."

Start a lecture with a bang, that's what Penelope's old biochemistry professor always said. After all, the universe began with one, why shouldn't you?

The quote achieved much the impact she'd imagined, but screw Einstein—the audience should take her word for it. The banner at the back entrance to the auditorium read:

Human Stupidity: Studies into Chlorovirus ATCV-1
A lecture by world renowned geneticist
Dr. Penelope Cooper

Pitching herself into the presentation, Penelope quickly cycled through a series of cartoon images on the PowerPoint screen:

Soldier with a gun.

"Humans fight repetitive wars…"

Click.

Woman worshiping in church.

"…believe all kinds of superstitious nonsense…"

Spin.

Confused man staring at blackboard etched with equation $E=MC^2$.

"…and still have trouble grasping the most basic scientific knowledge."

Whirl.

Penelope: "For a while we haven't been sure why. Is it poor education? Social factors? Genetics? Are we just extremely limited violent primates?"

At the back of the room Penelope noticed a young man dressed impeccably in a navy suit edge forward towards an empty chair. A frown creased her forehead at the distraction.

"Is this taken?" the man asked the woman occupying the adjacent seat.

"Today we know," Penelope declared. "It's Chlorovirus ATCV-1, the recently discovered *stupidity virus."*

"No, go right ahead," the woman said.

The man sat staring ahead grimly.

"You're familiar with Dr. Cooper's work?" the woman asked. "She's one of the most intelligent people in the world."

"I know stupidity," the man said without lifting his eyes off the lectern.

"Research shows ATCV-1 impairs cognitive ability and negatively impacts human intelligence. Large numbers of the human population are infected—current estimates suggest occurrence as many as 70% of the population may be diagnosed as clinically stupid. My team's work has been focused for the past two years on finding a cure. Today I can reveal we've made substantial progress with a trial vaccine which has increased the intelligence of a lab animal infected by the virus—"

Penelope turned to a table beside the lecture, empty but for a blue plastic cage. Opening the rear of the cage she produced a ginger British Shorthair cat. He sat blinking vacantly as she stroked his head.

"Ladies and gentleman let me introduce you to Stupid. A cruel name perhaps, but he was a very brainless cat. Not so anymore. Stupid, what is 2 + 2?"

Chairs squeaked and positions shifted as people leaned forward expectantly to peer at the cat.

Meow, meow, meow, meow.

"As you can see Stupid has begun to learn simple arithmetic. We hope this is just the beginning."

Stupid blinked again before lifting his leg to embark on a particularly enthusiastic preening session—beginning (and ending) with his balls.

At the after-function guests milled around—snacking, slurping, chatting—embarking on the post-event social activities that always made Penelope anxious. She poured herself a glass of water from the cooler.

"You must stop."

She turned around and there was the fine young man in the navy suit.

"I'm sorry? Mr…?"

"Jones. Toby. CEO. Chiefbridge Inc. Perhaps you know my work? Toby handed over his card which Penelope stared at blankly. "You must stop yours."

"Well, I've heard of you..." she stammered, "but I don't understand..."

"The stupidity virus is man-made Miss Cooper. It was created by vast corporations working alongside world governments. The purpose—simple—to keep society stupid, keep them good little consumers who don't ask questions. Stupid people spend more on stupid things and vote for stupid people. Can you imagine what a disaster you would cause to the status quo if the public began thinking? We'd have riots... who knows where that could lead... wealth equality... environmental harmony... civilization, even. That wouldn't do."

Penelope threw the contents of her glass in his face. "Nobody interferes with my work Mr. Jones." Turning on her heels, she walked off leaving him standing in an expanding pool of water.

"Stupid," Toby muttered. "Very stupid."

When she arrived at her research lab the following morning Penelope found men in blue uniforms emblazoned with the logo of *Happy Storage* packing everything away into boxes.

"What's going on?" she cried waving hands, shaking fists. "Hey be careful with that," she grabbed an industrial jaw crusher off a startled workman.

"Sorry, Penelope. Orders from above," Dr. Simpson, the center supervisor tried to comfort her. "Funding has been pulled and the lab's been closed. Your research assistants have been reassigned."

Throwing the jaw crusher into the supervisor's arms, Penelope punched a blue-clad mover in the stomach as he reached for the blue cage resting on the counter. *That wasn't clever,* she thought, *but it sure felt good!*

"No, not that one!"

Meow?

Stepping off the pavement with Stupid in her arms Penelope narrowly avoided being hit by a car.

"Look where you're going dumb-ass!" the driver shouted shaking his fist.

People are so rude, she thought.

Stupid sat on a bench in Penelope's basement lab watching with an expression approximating amusement as she rushed through the small space to the sink carrying a burning beaker.

"Of course Erbium can ignite in water," she said, wiping her forehead. "Why didn't I remember that?"

Meow.

Penelope looked at Stupid.

"I've been infected with the virus, haven't I? The guy at the lecture. What was his name? Tony? He spiked my drink with ATCV-1. It's the only explanation for what's happening to me."

Stupid curled up on a pile of paper. Clearly this was going to be a long night.

Penelope poured over her notes, pressing hand to forehead in frustration. “I’ll never be able to re-create the vaccine from my transcripts. I’m just no longer smart enough.”

From his vantage point, the cat opened one eye and seemed to sigh. “Take the genetic material from ATCV-1 that codes for the protein coat and insert that material into the skeleton of another virus. Isn’t it obvious?”

Penelope looked up with surprise. “Stupid you can talk!”

Stupid shrugged. “Sure, I’ve been able to talk for months. I chose not to.”

“Oh. That’s great!” She paused for a moment. “Look, I’m sorry about your name and treatment.”

“Who cares about a name? I don’t mind what you call me. I was a lab animal, and all that goes with that. I get it. Let’s put all that aside and work together on the vaccine.”

Penelope joyfully threw her arms around Stupid.

“Quit the cuddles, huh?” he hissed. “I’m a tough animal. Show me some respect.”

Working under Stupid’s direction Penelope quickly developed a new vaccine and administered it to herself. Then came time for an IQ test. Stupid tapped a computer key with his paw, waiting patiently for the results.

“How’d I do?” Penelope asked.

“123. It’s rapidly returning to normal. Soon you’ll be a genius again.”

Penelope moved to embrace Stupid before his serious, firm eyes met hers—stopping her dead in her tracks.

"Look, there's something I want to talk to you about too Penelope. I'm as tired of stupid people as you are. Let's cure them all."

"No more stupid people? That would be amazing!"

"All you need to do is put it in the water supply, then everyone will be smart as you are."

Penelope bent down and poured a concentrated vial of the vaccine into the large water treatment pond. She began to hum a new song she'd heard in the mall. Ariana Grande. It was good. Catchy tune. Awesome lyrics.

Scream.

Holding tightly to Toby's business card Penelope walked happily to his office, oblivious to the sounds in the street.

Smash.

I can't wait to tell him I've beaten his virus, she thought.

Crunch.

Traffic drove into traffic. Humans walked into humans. Humans walked into traffic. Traffic drove into humans. Amid the carnage, a twentysomething guy, face planted in phone, scratched his head at the plot intricacies of the latest Marvel movie. A naked woman walked up and down with a sign that read: "Vote Jesus!" A bucket-head (that's a guy with a bucket on his head) walked into a lamp-post. You get the chaos.

It was the next morning.

Outside the offices of Chiefbridge Inc. stood a huge sign reading Chiefbridge Inc. The security guard tired of his job, had decided to play Russian roulette. He placed his automatic weapon to his temple as Penelope stopped to ask directions. "Can I see Toby the CEO?"

"Sure. What the fuck? Go on up. He's on the twentieth floor."

She thanked him, turning away as the gunshot rang out.

"So I've done it," Penelope informed Toby. "No more stupid people."

Toby was much less interested than she'd expected.

"Sorry," he said grabbing his coat off a chair. "Late for a meeting. I have to fly."

Toby jumped out the window.

"It's the cat," Penelope thought. "His vaccine has made people more stupid. I'm gonna kill the cat."

Outside Penelope looked around confused. Every street seemed the same. And what was with all the tomato paste over the sidewalk? The city cleaners just weren't doing their job. People sucked thesedays. She looked around and saw an S sign. *S for safety.*

Down in the subway.

It seemed she had fucked up. She couldn't really remember anymore what it was that she had done, but people were always bitching at her. Making her feel small. Just one little mistake. Work politics, huh? What she needed was something to distract her. That's it. A device she could stare at all day and take her away from the reality of life. But who would invent such a thing? Maybe she would. After all she was a genious, write?

This thinkin waz mking her head hurt. Lozl. nIs music wen she gets om. Help her chill. K-pop, sure. Baby, baby, baz. Nicki Minaj. Why not? Haha. Jamz Blake. Nice. Auto tune is so gud. 1 directN. Gud. Kanye. d best. Absolutely. None of this wenk. A kewl mvie 2. Nothin boring. Or forein. Avenzers. Yeah. Anyfing with lotz of 3D. That's the bzt. Or explozions. No mor wrkin mi azz of.

Penelope climbed onto the tracks.

But… whr do I liv? whch way 2 go. pRhaps it's dwn DIS nIs tunnel. wot pritE lyts n d distanz!

Which just leaves Stupid.

"Don't call me Stupid."

6

THE LAST BEAT

The sea spray stings her eyes; wiping away tears, Elza Brown's vision blurs. *Arioka* disappears momentarily as the zodiac dips beneath the crest of another wave. Overhead: boomerang whirl; a flash and deafening explosion rips the cold pacific sky. "Look out!" Elza sees a metallic object shriek by. Then the swell takes them again. Elza falls back into Joey's lap, his hands close tight on her shoulders.

With deadly accuracy the harpoon strikes the grey whale in a spray of foam and flesh as the grenade head detonates. The water surges; then a whirlpool of boiling blood. The steel harpoon cable pulls tight, slicing across the water like a guillotine; if she reaches out her arm she could touch it.

Elza raises her head. Too far aft for an instant kill. The sea settles for a moment, a still and disquieting silence, before the wounded whale summons his final reserves of energy and begins towing the 750ft Arioka, against the drag of the winch, against the whirl of the propeller...

The *Ocean Warrior* had been trailing the whaler for two days, since it was picked up off the coast of Taiwan. Arioka had been operating since the early seventies, under various names, different countries, dubious ownerships, leaving a bloody trail across the pacific. The Japanese Whaling Commission denied any knowledge of her existence, even though most of the ship's catch ended up fetching top dollar in Tokyo's most exclusive restaurants. Arioka was a ghost ship, answerable to no one.

Almost no one.

Elza Brown joined the Warrior in London, its last port of call. She had been working there for the preceding eighteen months as an environmental correspondent for the Times. She met Captain Joey Alexander while covering the Ocean Warrior's research into pollution in the North Sea, and one thing led to another.

She watches him; his features gripped with grim determination as he spins the zodiac back towards the whaler, and knows what it was she saw in this plaintive man, almost twenty years her senior. A dashing roguishness to his appearance, an almost piratical air. She admires his blunted idealism, his own frustrated realization in the fruitlessness of his efforts, but his unswerving resolve to make a gesture regardless.

"Lots of people say what we do is futile, that there's no way of halting the rising tide of human destruction on the planet. But I don't care. I do it because it's the right thing to do. I don't think about winning or losing." It was her twenty-ninth birthday, and he smiled at her across the table taking notes. Elza looked around the busy London pub and blushed—and knew then she'd sleep with him that night.

A second harpoon rockets overhead; seconds later another explosion. It takes pieces out of the back of the whale, but does not kill him—the grenade must detonate inside the chest cavity for that small mercy. The odds against accuracy on a target, bobbing in the deep swells, immense. The grey whale plays out his last ounces of strength in a hopeless battle.

The other two Ocean Warrior zodiacs close in, continuing to harry the whaler, cutting to and fro across her bow, and as they do, Joey turns to stern. Elza holds on for dear life, the tiny inflatable rising dramatically in the artificial swells. She knows what he intends and has no fear in the knowledge. This is what she wanted after all—to make a difference, to make news, not write about it. She only hopes that the film crew back on the Warrior are getting the footage.

At the rear of the vessel, the ramp has been lowered to raise the dying animal aboard and begin butchery—it remained far more economic to select only the prime meat and discard the rest into the sea—than waste time processing it in entirety. It's Joey's plan to launch them aboard the ramp, and block the whale's ascent. It would make dramatic viewing on the six o'clock news. A veteran of many Greenpeace campaigns, Joey had learned early the value of good propaganda.

Activity on the ship's deck as they come around for a final approach. A handful of crewmembers gather at the railing. Catcalling, shouting abuse? No, they raise an object to the edge. Elza can't see what it is... and then it's let go... falling. The first dips harmlessly into the water—and is taken in undertow beneath the huge vessel's stern—by then the crewmen have had time to toss a second and a third. The metal oil barrels spiral end over end into their path. So quickly that Joey has no opportunity to swerve or pick up speed. He cries out her name, but she has no time even to answer.

Striking the front of the zodiac, the third barrel's impact sends boat and crew flying into the air. The zodiac flips twice, and Elza is lost in a spray of surf. She hits the water head first, driven down like a bullet, and for a few seconds, loses consciousness. Water surges, filled with cries.

When I was a little girl my father took me hunting.

We grew up outside Kerikeri, a small community in the Bay of Island's farming district. My father was as straightforward as my feelings for him were complex. A simple man who wanted to include his daughter in his life as much as his son. I think he felt some guilt at my mother not being around, as I did.

He wanted to make that up to me.

I remember a mist cloaked morning, with frost on the ground. I remember us trekking across the fields in heavy boots. Jordan running far ahead of us, as he always did. Ten years old then, I think my younger brother. I had just turned twelve.

Rabbits are a scourge, I know that. My father told me that (six years on a farm you know?)

We reach a field and the earth moves alive. It's not even sport. Jordan takes his shot, a miss, only seconds before they hide and then reappear, then it's my turn.

My father hands me the shotgun. He's shown me how to shoot at targets in the past, but this is different. It feels uncommonly heavy and I can't line up the sights. My father takes my hand in his to steady the gun. His hands are strong and crisscrossed with lines. I feel close to him as he whispers comforting instructions.

I aim high and pull the trigger.

When Elza opens her eyes, she's rising, enveloped in a cascade of foam. She can't breathe, her arms flailing desperately. Breaking the surface, she gasps for air, bobbing in the swell, directionless, searching for the comforting shapes of the Ocean Warrior or the satellite zodiacs—to no avail.

Blood in the water. A horrifically familiar shape floating close. The harpooned whale lies not ten meters away. The creature is bleeding so profusely that the water around it has turned a sickening roseate. A viscosity which reminds Elza of the oil slicks on Canadian beaches after the Exon spill. She moves her arms slowly in the thick liquid, gulps and spits water tainted with blood.

Her first intention is to get away, to escape the horror, but something other than the swirling waves draws her closer to the dying whale. She lets the tide take her, wash her. She wants to be there in his moment, to not let him be alone in death. His skin is warm and oily, the blood flowing from the gaping wound in his side, hot in her hand. A helpless despair, as the creature's eye turns toward and—he looks at her.

And what can she say in that moment? I'm sorry? I'm with you? I tried to stop this happening? A thousand emotions tug at her heart, none of them coalescing into anything permanent. She feels a connection to the creature, to his life and to his death. He feels it too—she instinctively knows he does. We have a common link? You're next, maybe? Is this it? She can't answer. She strokes the flipper, hanging tight to it as she watches the huge intelligent eye glaze over, and senses the moment life leaves his body.

Treading water, Elza begins to cry and thinks, *I am lost and lonely upon the ocean with this dead whale.* Stomach empty and soul too.

It's impossible for her to tell how much time passes before the sound of the zodiac engine stirs her to reality (a minute? five?). Shivering more due to shock than cold, she can barely assist the hands pulling her aboard.

Joey waits on the Ocean Warrior. He puts his arm around her, touching her hair matted with blood. It's only when she tries to stand on her own Elza knows something's seriously wrong. She sways, the deck swirls; she feels blood and bile rise up in her stomach, and then expel. Arms reach out, catching her before she falls. Then thankfully darkness claims her once again.

Flashes; hazy visions swimming on the edges of fever-sleep. A rolling cabin. Eggbeater. Blades whirl, and she rises, spinning by the wind. Lights flare, a dazzling warm glow. A nurse opens curtains. Elza tries to move her hand and a pain shoots through it. There's an IV drip in her wrist. The room too white. Blinking her eyes, she struggles to focus.

"When I was a little girl... we were in a car accident and my parents left me in a hospital overnight... I thought they'd abandoned me..." The past a collage of memory, leading her back to the present. A dull ache behind her temples, sleep drowsiness, and a question:

"Where am I?"

"In hospital."

The nurse turns reassuringly away from the window; a young Asian girl, a few years her junior. *I'm no longer young*, she thinks suddenly.

"You've been through an ordeal. You should rest."

"Where's Joey? The others?"

"You're lucky. You were winched off a couple of days ago. Your ship only arrived in port this morning."

"Has he been to see me? Have I missed him?" *Goodness, that sounds desperate*, she thinks.

"No one's been in yet. They've been busy with the media. The Chinese authorities want to impound your boat. Your accident made quite a stir..."

"It did?"

"He sent you a message. Joey—your boyfriend?"

"Yeah."

The nurse hands her a nondescript sealed envelope. Inside, the note reads simply: *Get well girl. I'll see you soon.*

Resolutely Elza folds the paper between her fingers. She folds it over and over again...

"What happened to me... I was in the water... and... the whale...?"

"You're suffering concussion. The doctor will be around soon. They're running some tests."

"What kinds of tests? What's wrong?"

"Oh blood—X-rays—the usual. Nothing to worry about!"

The room melts to silence as the nurse leaves. Elza wants suddenly to know her name. The sun is coming up across the streets of Hong Kong.

The voices of the marketplace mingle into one laborious drone. Elza wanders alone past the colorful stalls, stopping occasionally to browse with slight interest. Sick of the hotel room—of well-meaning people telling her to rest and recuperate. Sick of this place.

What she wants, Elza suddenly realizes is to go home. But where's that? London?

No, she wants to go back to New Zealand.

She has returned, naturally, over the years—a mother there still, a father, a brother's grave, but it's been a while this time—almost four years. The visits are fleeting, always like she's taking time out, and following a duty to see them. and always with the hidden desire to get back to her life. She did have her own life, after all…

Elza wishes she had someone to talk to. Joey's busy, trying to save his ship from confiscation. He's spent a single night with her in the five days since she left the hospital.

It's a cold aloof city to walk alone. Distant buildings and people. She remembers visiting as a journalist before the Chinese takeover. It seems like there's much less hope today... for the Hong Kong residents. Unemployment's rising, people are being paid less to work longer hours—and no one wants to talk to you anymore. Especially foreigners—it's like they feel betrayed.

Elza finds herself at the waterfront, without knowing why. Not difficult to find the Ocean Warrior; it's docked at the far end of a distant pier, which she makes her way along. There's a Chinese official at the gateway to the ship, but she flashes him her press card and a $100 note and he slips away to have a smoke.

On board it's silent, far quieter than she remembers. The soundless corridors cause her to shiver. An easy swaying motion, and odd creak come from beneath the old ship's deck. It makes her feel oddly queasy. She makes her way to the cabin she shares with Joey. Is she in love with him she wonders? Probably not. Has she ever been in love with any man? She enjoys men, but love?

Laughter at the corridors' end. She had thought the boat deserted. Treading closer, she's careful not to make a noise. Outside Joey's cabin, she hears his voice, and suddenly, a woman's. Pausing for a moment she ponders, touching the door handle lightly with her fingertips—then turns it.

They look up: Joey and the nurse from the hospital. The girl is on top of him, naked, and seems the most embarrassed, reaching for a sheet to cover her small, thin body. Joey smiles—damn him, all charm, so good looking. "Hi, El... uh I think you know Susan…. sorry I should have told you."

"Yeah, you should," she replies calmly.

"So... want to join in?"

Susan smiles awkwardly, the sheet slips off her shoulder, a flash of skin. Elza steps inside and closes the door.

Airports are no fun, no fun at all.

Crowds, sweaty tourists, children running around, queues...

Elza arrives at Auckland airport's terminal. Lines of people wait to greet their loved ones off the Hong Kong sourced flight, but no one for Elza.

She taps lightly against the window of the first taxi and the driver climbs out to help her with her suitcase. Elza seats herself in the back and the car pulls away. The driver asks her destination.

She feels like vomiting. A hotel. Any good hotel.

Auckland City. She remembers as a child coming here with her parents and being in awe of the size and scope of it all—but it's rather small in comparison isn't it? When you've been to New York, Paris, London... it puts everything in perspective.

A re-run of *That '70s Show's* playing on a station and she watches the screen with the volume muted. Somehow the childhood nostalgia depresses her. From the hotel room, Elza watches the lights of the city flare and die. She pours herself another drink staring at the tinctured card from a pregnancy test.

She gets up and walks to the window.

All she wanted when she left was to get away, and to try and make the world a better place. Make a better place for children. What had she achieved really? A week ago she watched men butcher a sentient creature and she was powerless to prevent it. She knows her faith in mankind diminishes day by day... powerless to prevent that too.

The phone rings. It's Susan.

"It's okay," Elza says. "I know why I'm feeling sick."

Susan passes her over to a doctor.

By the time Elza arrives home in Kerikeri she knows she's dying. Multiple myeloma, also known as plasma cell myeloma, a cancer of plasma cells. Twelve months, the doctor on the phone explains. Get your affairs in order. That's it. Time ran out.

It should shake her more, but after the initial shock she feels a strange calmness. She doesn't intend to tell her mother. It's not something you do after four years: turn up on the person who brought you into this world's doorstep and say: "Hi Mum, guess what—I'm going to die—there's no hope."

At least not this woman...

Alone in life. Alone in death. There's not much to say to people on the periphery.

"Hello Dad," Elza says.

"Oh it's you," her father squints as if through a drug and alcohol haze. "The prodigal daughter. Long-time no see."

"Sorry. I've been busy."

Elza waits for a moment to be asked in, and steps inside after hesitation when she realizes she may not be.

"Have you seen your mother?"

"I called in before I came here; she was out."

The room's mostly tidy, dismissing the dishes in the sink, and the empty spirit bottles collecting by the dustbin. A stereo's blaring Fleetwood Mac; her father reaches for a remote to turn it down. Elza sinks into a thread worn couch.

"I saw one of your stories in *Time*. Your mother showed me," her father looks up. "You could let me know when stuff is coming out—I still take an interest you know."

"I know—I meant to send you copies... I keep meaning to."

"Well I know you. I know you're here to try and make yourself feel better that you're fulfilling your duty to your parents. But it can't go on. I like being alone."

"Dad—that's not why I'm here."

"I don't know why you're here. Well I do. You're
pregnant
aren't you?"

"What? How do you know? How could you?"

"I can tell. You look the same way your mother looked."

"I don't know what to say...."

"Who's the father? You don't love him do you?"

"Stop it Dad! You can't read my mind!"

"She could!" He offers her a joint and shrugs. "No, you don't, do you?"

Elza holds out her hand.

"Changing ways eh?"

"Yeah, changing ways."

Elza climbs back in her rental car; lightheaded, she drives back to the motel, locks the car and starts walking.

Kerikeri.

It's hardly changed a bit in all these years, Elza thinks, threading her way through the town's quaint streets. Twilight draws in, and memories too. All those nights with different boys, when she'd go out and find her way home by moonlight, or make love under stars. She feels the lure of those times even more acutely tonight. Tonight when she knows she's dying, and she should feel fear, or sadness, she's only restless. There's a seeming aimlessness to her peregrination. An aimlessness that until now has had no destination.

She turns suddenly into Orange Grove Road and there it is. The sense of déjà vu is quite profound as she begins to walk down the street where she grew up. She passes number six where her best friend Kelly lived. The house has been painted; green, it was white for so long. The little shrub out the front—now a tree. Elza pauses for a moment, half expecting to see a blond-haired schoolgirl rush down the steps to meet her. She heard Kelly went overseas. She hasn't seen or thought of her in years. Or any of her school friends for that matter. Elza keeps going, down the rows of suburban houses. She wonders if any of the same people still live in them? There's one house on the street where she knows the inhabitants have long gone: number 24. *The number of times I wrote this address,* she thinks, *it followed my name on a thousand letters and forms 'till I was seventeen.* So many firsts here. I had my first birthday here. First walked here. First laughed. First cried. First had sex. First learned about loss here...

For a moment she doesn't know what she's doing, then she's walking up the path. Her mother's little circular garden where the red roses grew has been filled in. Those roses had been there since Elza could remember. When she was small, when she was outside with her mother, she used to snap the thorns off the branches and stick them to her nose like a rhinoceros. There are other things missing, but Elza's too preoccupied to notice; she sees children playing on the front lawn and hears the sounds of tiny laughter.

Reaching the front door, she knocks. *Strange; this must be almost the first time she's knocked on this door in her life.* An athletic young Māori man answers the door. Behind him a little boy runs past, a blur with a toy airplane in his hand. For a second Elza finds herself lost for words. She doesn't really know why she's here or what she should say.

"Hello," she says at last. "Um... this may sound really dumb, but I used to live here years ago—I grew up in this house. I was wondering if I could have a look around?"

The man seems taken back at first, but then his mouth melts slowly into a smile. "Sure. Come in."

"You don't mind?" Elza steps into the hallway.

"No, no—not at all. You'll just have to excuse the mess—my wife's in hospital—she's expecting," he waves his hand in a sweeping motion over his stomach, "and I haven't had time to tidy up after Ben."

He's exaggerating, Elza thinks. Okay, it isn't as immaculate as her mother kept it, but the house is no greater mess than she'd expect from a couple with a small child. Lego scattered indiscriminately; she's careful not to step on twin plastic dinosaurs on the lounge floor. She recognizes the carpet as the spiral red and black design her mother bought when Elza started high school. She always hated that carpet. Wallpaper has changed though.

"You probably want to be alone," the man says. "You go ahead and have a look at what you want. I'll just be out there," he goes to the kitchen where he begins preparing tea. Elza thanks him and makes her way silently through the rooms. To her mother's room, where the memories are dullest. She hardly ever entered this room when she lived here. There was something about her mother which never invited the closeness that should have been.

In her old bedroom, the past is nearer. It has been made up for the baby; a bassinet in one corner, near a single bed. The walls have been freshly painted in neutral cream; an acrylic waif slightly taints the air. Elza sees the echo of her own furniture; in her mind it's still her room. Her bed used to face a big white dressing table where she spent hours sitting in front of the mirror, worrying about the shape of her nose or a new pimple that had suddenly appeared. She sits down on the small bed placed exactly where her old bed had been. There used to be a stuffed toy animal who, after she had grown out of taking him to bed, had lived his life on the dresser. A fox. She doesn't have it anymore. She wonders if her mother does?

The backyard with its colorful fruit trees reminds her of summers spent outdoors, playing in the sandpit or swimming pool, or later when she lay out in a bikini, trying to get a tan. She remembers the dear pets she lost at this address. Two were buried here. Her last, and favorite, was a Siamese cat named Devon; she follows the fence line and finds the place immediately. After she died, they planted a maple on her grave. The tree's still there, and so she assumes is Devon the cat. She kneels down for a while in silence at the cat's grave before going inside.

The new owner, whose name she discovers is Dennis, and who has lived in the house for the past three years, invites her to stay for a cup of tea. At first she refuses, not wanting to impose further, but when he insists she agrees and sits with him at the kitchen table. It turns out he's excited to talk to someone about the impending birth of his second child. He's hoping for a girl.

"I hope so too," Elza sips black tea. "It'd be nice to have a little girl around this house again."

"So what brings you back here?" Dennis asks.

"I don't know—to the town? I'm not really sure," she replies.

"Do you know about salmon?" he asks.

"Salmon?"

"Yeah, they live in the ocean all year, but then, in winter, they feel an uncontrollable urge to swim back to the same place they were born."

"I've heard of that. To spawn and die. I wonder why they do it?"

"I guess they just have to. Like all of us."

7

FIREFLIGHT

Halcyon Girl frolics dolphin-like in the updrafts, letting one gust take her, rising buoyantly, before slipping back to catch another.

A dramatic sunset soon. Tangerine muted off-white clouds melting, drifting into ice-cream nothingness. Pyramid City stretches below, a labyrinth, a rough diamond cut of polished gray gems. People scurry from work in slow ant-trails, returning to their cozy, safe nests. Freeways are grid locked. Nobody seems worried. A lazy summer weekday evening where nothing will happen. Watchers below might mistake her, dressed in her gaudy lemon-yellow costume, for an aerobatic bi-plane or a late-season firefly. A firefly that knows time is running out. *Mate,* it thinks. *Mate for that is all you exist for. That is all you are.*

Fresh currents of air lap at her bare skin; legs, arms and belly. The costume admittedly covers little. She feels caressed and immediately aroused, erect nipples protruding through sheer Spandex. The same sensation coalesces between her legs. She touches herself and realizes she's wet. Could she masturbate up here in the clouds? Who would notice? Perhaps Atomic Man or Wolf Gal would swing by? She smiles at that thought. Or worse, Dr. Haunt, her man-in-the-mask nemesis hatches another scheme while she's caught mid-coitus. Very unbecoming for any self-respecting superheroine.

No, tonight the carnal pleasures that await her are upon Earth. The memory of his kiss still lingers. Ironic that even after tantric intergalactic escapades, flings with superheroes and heroines, virtual-deities, so near perfection, it's David who excites her; one man whom she's drawn to beyond any other—and he's just a normal man.

Well, almost normal.

The firefly enjoys a last swoop; the turbulence, worsening, a chill waver from the ocean. She jumps a current, as if a high diving platform, somersaults, ending her aerobatics upright, and allows herself to fall away, boots first, towards the rushing earth.

Cries below as she descends. A crisis. They are drowning. Screaming. Scattered in the shallows along the golden beach. Her libido has to wait, danger calls—like a bush fire on the horizon casting a red glow into the night. Adults and children, crying in fear and pain as the unknown hand of death reaches for them. The ground is coming up fast, but she doesn't slow; sand deadens a heavy landing.

Save my child.

Help me.

Kill me.

Singing voices muddled and mixed up. And something else. The pod of pilot whales, disorientated, dead mingling with living. Blood on sand. Acoustic-induced hemorrhages. *I want to get home... but...*

A sound reverberates, invisible on the horizon, imperceptible to human ears. Halcyon Girl isn't quite human. *It hits me: I'm in this world to help.*

At an amplitude of two hundred and forty decibels: low frequency active sonar of the type used by the military to detect submarines. Loud enough to kill cetaceans.

A whoosh of breeze.

"I can see it," Atomic Man drops beside her. "Freedom-class littoral combat ship if I'm not mistaken."

"Well, do something!" Halcyon Girl cries. "I'll float the living off the sand bar."

"Do something?" Atomic Man toys with his beard.

"Stop the navy sonar!"

"I used my atomic vision to jam the sonar exactly 3.0125 seconds ago."

Halcyon Girl listens. *Oh, he's right.*

"Although different isotopes, sound is made up of atoms in much the same way that traffic is made up of cars. It's a simple task for me to disrupt any mass at the sub-atomic level."

Atomic Man can be such a dick sometimes.

Leapfrogging between the mammals, Halcyon Girl implores them to remain calm, reiterates she's here to help; echoing this they call out, each reassuring the other. Ploughing through the sandy beach, Atomic Man digs a channel from the whales to the deeper ocean. Halcyon Girl nudges the first whales into it.

Hundreds of people stand watching—from the top of the dunes down to the water. “Are you going to save the whales?” a little girl nearby asks.

“Well, we’re going to give it our best shot and given the amount of support I don’t think we can fail!”

Halcyon Girl rocks one whale from side to side to get her used to motion again. Waves draw closer. The stranded pilot whale has been so calm the whole time… Halcyon Girl can’t imagine how scary it must be… out of her natural element and surrounded by a crowd of weird looking creatures. The whale keeps her eyes open, her breathing steady. *She knows…*

Waves arc higher and higher.

A cottage is planted on the outskirts of Pyramid city, close enough to the ocean, that with the wind in the right direction you can sit on the veranda and enjoy the scent of salt spray, sand, and sweet dried driftwood. The front door’s ajar and his car’s in the driveway. Beaten her home once again. David has the luxury of a stable job, a successful startup boss, he can pick his own hours. The clash of lifestyles comes in strange moments.

Like this, as Halcyon Girl turns a pilot whale gently toward open ocean. Or when she treads along metal corridors; the latest lair of Dr. Haunt—Halcyon Girl’s plate metal-masked enemy—enemy of all superheroes, or when she thwarts a bunch of bungling bank robbers who choose the wrong city for their get-rich-quick schemes… in such moments she wonders: what’s David doing? How does an executive in a software company spend his day?

Demanding and perfection-seeking in his personal life, she imagines him being this way at work: a Steve Jobs boss from hell. What if he's the opposite? She'd sure like to be a fly on the wall of his office. It occurs to employ Invisible Lad to follow him for a day and report back, but she quickly dismisses it. She loves and trusts David too much for that. Also, she's quite a catch—who else has a girlfriend who fights crime (and saves whales) in a costume resembling a lemon swimsuit?

"You're almost there, let it go."

Clapping from the crowd as the whale moves off with a flick of the tail.

It's the easiest part, to let go.

Other surviving cetaceans follow, slicing through waves past the waist deep vividly-costumed super humans; the pod reassembles, orientates, and navigates into deeper water.

The crowd cheers, and they, superstars, take a bow.

"I will not forget their cries," Halcyon Girl sniffs tearfully. Atomic Man diffidently slides his arm around her shoulder.

"Such is life," he admits, looking down at her transparent-wet costume.

David steps onto the porch, a beer in his hand, something unreadable in his eyes, something a suddenly aching heart wants to believe is hers for the asking. "Hello Lucy," he watches her carefully. "How was your day?"

Yes, here on Earth, she's Halcyon no more. Just plain Lucy.

"Not so bad. I saved some whales in the evening and defeated *Ultimax: The Ultimate Thinking Machine* before lunch."

"How was that?"

"Not so difficult. I asked him why is bra singular and panties plural? He said he needed to sit on the pavement for a minute and think about it. I believe he's still there."

"Of course," David smiles, sipping his beer; rugged, deep and sexy in an intellectual kind of way. Suddenly all Lucy wants is for him to lead her upstairs and strip her.

"We can now, if you like?" His beautiful New England accent makes her shiver.

"It's not fair you can do that, you know," she replies.

"Do what? Drink my beer?"

"No," she looks up at him, changing her face into what she hopes is its most neutral expression. "It's not fair you can read my mind."

"Well," he smiles. "A guy has to use all the tricks he has in his book to stay ahead, doesn't he?"

Lucy strides to him, and his hand naturally slides to her thigh.

"Shut up," she replies, playfully pushing him against the cottage wall. He collides a little hard and she apologizes. She has to control her strength around normal humans. Once when they were enjoying rough sex in the bedroom, she inadvertently put him through a wall.

"I can't hide my thoughts, but you can't hide who you are. All your deepest emotions, your loves and fears are open to me David. I know who you are inside."

She feels it now, a little fear. There at the beginning of their relationship. It took time to close the distance between them. It must not have been easy for him. He had perhaps dreams of the picket fence and the wife who dutifully bears him two point five children, but that wasn't ever going to be Lucy. She's the firefly of the skies.

He smiles, whatever he sees in her mind reassures him. The wrinkle on his brow softens. "I am a little afraid of you at times. It's not just your strength, the physical differences in what we are. I don't do it often, but sometimes I spend time in your mind and everything is so complex and vast it leaves me feeling small and insignificant. You're a superheroine Lucy!"

"I didn't know you were so afraid." Lucy moves close enough to draw warmth from his body. "My powers must be not so great as I believed they were."

They smile together at this, at the super-human's fallibility.

"Come upstairs with me?" Lucy asks.

"Will you carry me?"

"No, I'm not Halcyon. I am Lucy."

Removing his hand from her pants he's down on his knees, tracing faint hair that runs down her belly. His wet fingers leave trails.

"Are you trying to kill me?" Lucy asks.

"No, I'm trying to fuck you, but you're still dressed."

Quickly remedying this, she stands before him, glimpsing herself in the dresser mirror; six-foot-tall, giraffe-long legs, ebony hair flowing down her back, a perfect Bernini carved in marble.

Orgasms rush in as an afterthought. Hands pressed tight. An inexorable ecstatic full stop. When Lucy closes her eyes she can only see the atoms of his, dancing within her. In a world of miracles, this is her miracle, here now and on earth.

The evening still young, they cook dinner as normal couples do. She asks if he can take her spare costume to the dry-cleaners tomorrow if he's going into the city? David nods. He tells her he's toying with the idea of mowing the lawn while it's still warm, while there's light. She asks if he will mow without a shirt, so she can come and watch. Anything's possible, he tells her.

The brick shed beckons him. It's only small. Big enough to store the lawnmower, a few tools and parts. She doesn't have the key and there's sure no need for her to have it. For a super-human with the fate of the world on their shoulders, who cares what's located in one, dark, grimy red brick shed at the end of the garden?

She could always break the lock anyway. Or the bricks. He considers this as he turns the key in the lock. But why would she? What has he to hide?

Inside, David gets out the lawnmower. Some spark plugs. In the tall metal locker that stands rather ominously in the corner. Only it's not covered with fine layers of dust and cobwebs. He opens the small, tinny, frail door. No spark plugs. He feels like looking. There. A black cloak. A tunic. Some tight-fitting brown pants. It would be ill-conceived of any self-respecting super-villain to choose anything other than earth tones. There it is. On a shelf. He reaches for the grim, battered plate metal mask. He holds it up to his face, and through the narrow slits, through light of the door can see Lucy calling him from the veranda.

Just a normal man. Well, almost.

8

SIMON SAYS

The wooden stick stirs slowly in dark coffee.

There's a container of wooden stirring sticks on a side stand in the cafe, along with raw sugar, real sugar and fake sugar. I put two sachets of real sugar in my coffee and stir it slowly with a wooden stirring stick. Then I pick up a handful of wooden stirring sticks and make my way to a table in the corner.

Breaking the sticks. Breaking the sticks. One by one. In half. Now they are all broken in two and scattered on the surface of the stained veneer table. Now I can begin building. I sip my coffee. It's good and I close my eyes, slipping away. All around me, the hum of voices recedes to nothing and there's just one voice.

Yes, the voice. The one voice. But not yet. I don't hear him yet. There are other voices first.

The psychiatrist's voice. He's in his late thirties; very handsome, and I am ever-so-slightly attracted to him. I don't like his voice though. What is it saying now? It's explaining about Major Depressive Disorder (this is what it thinks I have). It's asking me questions, and I am mumbling replies to keep the voice happy. The voice asks if I feel like my mood has been up and down and I don't know the answer.

Other voices; muddled voices, overlapping each other, vicious tides trying to pull me under.

It's the voice of Jared my boyfriend. It's telling me he loves me. I love Jared, but he's a liar. I hate Jared.

It's the voice of my mother screaming at me. Literally screaming; a wailing banshee, red face, eyes stabbed black plugs in wrinkled skin. I try to focus: it sounds like: *Rachel, you can't eat it.*

I'm not sure. What did I eat? A wooden stirring stick?

Jared now. It sounds like: *stupid teenage slut—you've ruined my life.* I listen again. It rewinds and replays in my mind, a very bad song. Oh. That's exactly what it was. That's what he said.

My mother again: *Rachel, you can't keep it.*

Crying. Drama. Crying. Drama. I find it hard to keep up. I feign emotion, but I'm not really emotional. I am the very opposite. I nod and agree until she calms down, and then she makes a call. I go along. What do I know? I am just a stupid teenage slut.

In the cafe a tower of wooden stirring sticks has appeared in front of me. I flatten it and leave. There's a splinter in my finger. Life is full of splinters.

I weather a busy week, full of classes and coursework, and almost forget that I am pregnant. The appointed day comes, and my mother and I visit the clinic. A friendly doctor, with a beard as white as his coat looks over my medical history briefly, and then proceeds with an ultrasound. All I can make out in the picture of my uterus (I peek after it's done) is a dark, ovoid shadow. He says that it's the developing fetus. That is all he needs to see to move forward. He books me in for another appointment in a week's time.

For the next few days I become obsessed with drawing fetuses. I fill notebooks with pencil etchings of their curled inert bodies. I draw one and color it red with felt-tip pens and email it to Jared. He never replies. He never asks how I am.

On a late summer afternoon which turns out to be the most humid of the year, I return to the clinic with my mother, and we are greeted by the doctor, a different one this time, though no less warm and friendly. It occurs to me suddenly why my mother is so keen for me to have an abortion—because she wishes she'd never had me. She wishes she'd had an abortion, sixteen years ago. There's a clock ticking somewhere, but I can't see it. I am nervous. I feel sick. I am going crazy.

Leading me into a sterile, white room, a nurse gives me a smock to change into, and tells me not to worry I won't feel anything.

She's right.

When it's over, I see only whiteness. Beyond these walls, there's a sudden commotion in the waiting room and the doctor and nurse excuse themselves, telling me to lie still. I sit up for a moment, and that is when I first hear the voice.

It's saying my name and coming from the sterile yellow plastic bin marked *Medical Waste.*

"Rachel." It's the voice, cooling and hypnotic. Calling.

I'm on my knees in front of the bin and the voice is louder, more urgency in tone. I think of flowers, yet all I smell is antiseptic. He tells me his name. His name is Simon. Simon says what I should do next. I open the lid and the world evaporates into whiteness.

The baby stroller is white. It's very expensive and I think the shop assistant has some doubts about my ability to pay, directing me to a cheaper model. What she doesn't know is I've got plenty of cash after shoplifting expensive bras and underwear from *Farmers* and selling them on *Trademe*. No, I explain. I want the best for my baby. What's the baby's name, she asks and I say: Simon.

Our first walk together. The sun warms my face and I feel so happy for the first time in a very long time. It's down to Simon. He makes me very happy and I tell him so. Simon smiles and says he's glad. Simon has a beautiful smile. He will be a heart breaker.

We walk together around the city. I show Simon my favorite places where I grew up, where he was born. It's a long tiring day for us, and I order a coffee and sit down at an outside table on the waterfront.

A couple of middle-aged women leave the cafe and glance in my direction. One smiles and they come over. She tells me she's a new grandmother and asks how old my baby is, and I tell her just a few days. They ask if they can see him, and I say yes. Of course, I would have said no if I'd known what their reaction would be. I don't expect them to scream in horror as they pull back the blankets in the stroller, but that's exactly what they do. They scream at Simon, and their horrid voices make him afraid, and he cries. Look. See what you've done—you've upset him. I lift Simon from under the blankets and hold him to me for protection. The large pickling jar feels warm in my hands and within it Simon the fetus swims freely in clean brown liquid.

A crowd's forming and there are more voices, but they are all talking at once and I can't make out what they're saying. People are shoving me and someone makes a move to reach for the glass jar. *No, I scream. He's mine!*

I push through the crowd and run from the waterfront, saline taste in my mouth, tears streaming. There's an alleyway and I walk down it. Dark and cold, surrounded by bricks on all sides. It feels safe and I slide down the wall behind a cold metallic jumbo bin. I am sobbing. *I'm sorry they don't like you. They think you're ugly or something, but it doesn't matter. I will always love you. I think you're beautiful. I will never leave you.*

Simon has his father's eyes. It makes me sad and I begin to cry more. Simon who's been silent for a while, asks what's wrong. I explain about his father—that he doesn't want a part in our lives. That he's cold and callous like the people today.

"Maybe we'll have to do something about him," Simon says. He plants the idea in my head, but it's Simon's idea.

Just as taking the large kitchen knife to Jared's flat is Simon's idea. Jared is older, a university student and has already hooked up with another girl. He's surprised to see me, yet invites me in. I sit on the edge of his bed, playing nervously with my dress, and place my bag on the floor. *So you got rid of it,* he asks. I don't reply, but he keeps talking. *But you got rid of it?* I don't know what it is, so I take the glass jar out of my bag and place it on a chair. Jared mutters something I don't hear. Perhaps he doesn't say anything. Perhaps he's just breathing.

His name is Simon, I explain. *Isn't he beautiful?*

"Kill him. Stab him. He's a worthless sack of shit. Cut his cock off and stick it in his mouth."

Jared tells me I am sick, fucked up, crazy. He tells me all these things, but it doesn't stop me doing what Simon tells me to do.

I hate my mother. I wish she was dead. I can only confide these things to Simon. Only he understands me. "Poison the old bat," Simon says.

My mother has the oddest expression as she lies on the floor amidst spilled coffee, foaming at the mouth, eyes wide staring. I think she's looking at Simon, but he doesn't want to see her, preferring to turn his back to her in his glass womb. I have the feeling he holds a grudge.

The authorities will come and separate us. No one understands.

"I love you," Simon says.

I love you so much and I know you love me.

"Don't worry—there's a place we can go," Simon says. "There's another world, a better world. I will show you."

We trek three days into the Urewera forest, where Simon says we will find a door. By then I have eaten the last Mars bar and have been feeling dizzy for the past few hours. I fill my water bottle up at a stream. At least there's water. We keep walking, but every tree and every fern look alike, and I can't help feeling we are going in circles. Simon stays positive and keeps me buoyant. He sings softly to me although I don't understand the words, they are majestic outer-worldly symphonies. Simon says the door is only a few hours away.

Time passes. I do not know how long. Simon has gone quiet. I begin to see things that aren't there. Māori tribesmen ripped from the 19th century, their cries stark, harsh and angry at me. My mother's face and Jared's, and a myriad of white coated herons. A nightmare blurred into daylight.

"I'm sorry," Simon says. "I can't find the door. You are dying. I have let you down."

No you haven't Simon, don't ever say that. You cannot let me down. You are perfect.

"You will die out here without food," Simon says.

But there's nothing to eat.

"No. There's something." The beautiful voice emanates from the pickled contents of the glass jar. Then Simon tells me what I must do.

At first, it fills me with horror, but an organism's survival instinct is strong and I always do what Simon says.

Afterwards, I lie on the cold ground and with something inside me; my thoughts begin to become clear for perhaps the first time in a while. I press my face to the soft earth. My hands reach to touch silvery wild lichen and my body stretches on the soft blanketing green of moss and rich fertile loam. I inhale everything around me. Wind in flickering leaves. A bird calls. Then all the sounds and lingering voices fade to nothingness. Smells of dirt and death and rebirth.

9

COWBOY & TRIBE

Heat rises in a shimmering desert. I stand on shifting sands. Dust and tumbleweed. I scan the open plains. The air arid; my mouth tastes of tobacco. Tethered to a tree, a horse whinnies; the click of metal at my hip. Sounds remind me who I am. Alive in spirit, at least.

Myth. Not dead.

Searching endlessly. Sensing something out there; nature and civilization colliding. Whispered on the soft trails of the wind, hinted at on steep mountain trails, heralded upon the open plains… moving from constraint into independence.

Individuality. Freedom. Words feeding the human dream.

A plank lifts underfoot as I step up from muddy, shit-strewn street and make my way towards the sheriff's office.

1875. Bodie, Texas—at the edge of the booming wild west frontier.

Ezra Gray. I hear my name travel, a murmured prayer among the townspeople gathering like locusts. Women in Sunday-best drag children by the arms along the main street towards me as if comforting rag toys. Curiosity moves to the two horses tethered to a hitching rail—one with a man tied motionless over the saddle.

Inside the office, I motion with my head for the sheriff and deputy to follow. "Here to claim the bounty on the Jackson brothers."

Cut down off the horse, the fugitive groggily gets to his feet—and alive—is taken into custody.

"This one didn't put up a fight—the other, did," I explain.

"I only see one Jackson brother," The sheriff says. "Reckon that gets you half the bounty."

"Not so fast."

A slow, deliberate gait as I make my way to the horses. Opening a saddle-bag I take out a course hemp sack stained crimson-black.

"Warrant said there was a bounty on both their heads—dead or alive." I toss the sack through the air. It lands with a sickening thud in the mud at the lawman's feet. "It was a long ride back. Figured I didn't really need the rest."

"You been out in the wild too long son," the sheriff says, shaking his head. "We act a little more civilized in this town."

A smirk crawls across my mouth. "The way I look at it—I done him a favor."

"How's that?"

"The best of all things is something entirely outside our grasp: not to be born, not to be, to be nothing. But the second best thing is to die soon."

Hush. Sherriff and deputy exchange dumbfounded glances while the crowd disperses.

"I'll arrange your blood money."

“I can wait,” I mutter. “Been riding a while. Like to get myself a drink, a bath, and some pussy first. Not necessarily in that order.”

“The Buckhorn’s just a block to your left. They got rooms. Bourbon’s good. Saloon girls are friendly and you’ll find a coral to freshen up your horses.”

I nod. Tumbleweed blows in from the prairie and scuttles down the street, skeletal footballs driven by ghosts.

“After more work?” The sheriff glances out the window. I follow his gaze. A dusty, windy day on offer. A good day to keep your head down, and stay indoors.

I stare at the wanted poster the sheriff slides forward on the counter. The image takes me back years. The American Civil War.

Back up a few hours.

“You’re sure a beautiful looking man,” the prostitute smiles tracing her fingers along my jawline. “I’d almost do you for free.”

Not one feature makes my face handsome, though perhaps my eyes come close. Blue, beautiful in any shade. From within burns a brutal strength. “That’s a very kind offer.” What I hide beneath is a deadly arrogance.

“Almost. $10.”

Steam lifts from the hot still sea of the polished steel bathtub. The room itself is simple, but clean. A wooden austerity which makes me for a moment, nostalgic. Wind tugs curtains at the window. A cigar in one hand, a glass of bourbon in the other I replay conversations in my mind.

“Ex-military, wanted throughout Texas for a string of robberies, murder and extortion. Goes by the name of El Capitán. He and his gang fled into Mexico.”

Captain Cornelius Cates.

“The reward?”

“The governor of Texas has put a $500 bounty on Cates, dead or alive.”

Placing the cigar firmly between my teeth, I reach for the wanted poster tucked beneath a dog-eared copy of *The Birth of Tragedy* on the side table. Scars lacerate the right side of the face in the black-and-white photograph.

The squeal of wheels on tracks changes tone. Battered, bruised and bleeding we face each other. The runaway train mounts a bridge. Cates makes a dive for the rifle on the floor. A shovel digs into the engine furnace. Red hot coal sprays Cates face. Screaming he stumbles backward…

“I’ll do it. Fee’s $1.”

Bodie slips slowly into darkness.

1862. Metal zips the air, ricocheting through tightly packed redwood trees.

“Lootenant, it’s a trap.”

Grey uniforms sink to earth as I motion my men to take cover. A foray along the Mississippi river to outflank the Union and ease pressure on the siege of Vicksburg. Ambush. Waiting. Lining the banks. Bark flies from trees. Blood bouquets sprout on summer grass.

“Back, into the woods,” I scream.

Life at breakneck speed… senses alert… colors vivid… heart pumping… and instinct kicks in. Form a defensive circle.

Navy blue movement through the trees. Surrounded. Men crying out. A killing ground. The platoon's being cut down. Surrounded. Better start thinking. Leading. Requesting reinforcements is impossible. It'll be dark soon. A chance to break out. A lull descends over the afternoon as both sides take stock.

Sergeant King drags a body. Northern prisoner. Young man. Barely. A kid. Almost. The boy breaks down. The Northerners knew we were coming. Waited in ambush most of the hot day, killing time.

"A traitor," the young man stammers. "Someone in Confederate high command. A spy working for the North in your midst."

"A name?" King demands; when met by silence, he beats the prisoner to no avail.

Boy's no one. Foot soldier. Here to die like us.

Limitless options in life take us to this one patch of ground, where our choices are whittled away to just a few: surrender, die, or attempt to break out.

Shadows lengthen between trees as dusk settles. Men blacken their faces and uniforms with mud. Wounded lie moaning; for them their fate is sealed. I order the worst cases shot; out of mercy, and practicality. There'd be little compassion from the North, and they'd only hold us up.

I give another order and we—a platoon of fifty mowed down to just a couple of dozen men—move out.

"Let me stay here," the Union prisoner sobs with fear as I tie a rope around his neck. "I ain't done nothing."

"You haven't done anything," I correct him, tightening the rope. "You're coming too. Way I figure it, if we get out of here, high command will take talk of a traitor a lot more serious direct from the horse's mouth."

He protests a little more till I beat him a little more.

Treading cautiously through the undergrowth, I trace our path back along the edge of the great river. Inevitably we come across enemy troops, and when we do, myself and a small squad form a rearguard: opening fire into trees at our concealed enemy. A Winchester 1860 holds sixteen rounds. Technology brings with it strength and the hint of the betterment of civilization. That the Winchester is the *Gun that Won the West* should come as no surprise. When is enough, enough? Will we know when civilization begins its slow slide into darkness as surely it must? What is our epoch? Still out there in the distance of time, out of reach? Or is this it?

I let off half my rounds before our area's pummeled with bullets. My squad's torn apart in seconds. Only I and the prisoner escape.

Soon we catch up to the survivors. I call out, but nervous, exhausted, and defeated, they open fire. The prisoner slumps against me, blanketing my body from friendly fire. I scream again and finally the shooting ceases.

"Lootenant!"

King's made it with a half-dozen infantrymen. "Are you okay?"

"I'll do."

The prisoner stares back vacantly, blood seeping from a neat circle in his chest. Little more than a teenager. Then, so am I.

I await execution in a dark, damp prison cell—the first in a block of six. New Orleans. There's something cowardly about an execution. Taking a man, hands tied, shooting or stringing him up. No matter what he's done, anyone deserves a fighting chance.

Scenes replay in a mind's eye.

"A traitor?" Colonel Humphries… my commanding officer. "Only very senior officers knew of the mission, and you, Ezra."

Quite a performance.

"Not one of your surviving men heard the Union prisoner's story," his adjutant Captain Cornelius Cates joins in the drilling down with glee.

My belongings are searched and among them, family letters are produced. Cates reads one: "I'm not ashamed to fight on the side of the Confederacy—a soldier fights for his country—right or wrong; Virginia is my State, and the South my country, yet even I doubt the political merits of the cause… for if I were to put myself in the shoes of the black man I would fight and die rather than be a slave."

It's enough to condemn me.

"Big nigger lover, huh Gray?" Cates asks. I know his kind. Gloating egotist from a wealthy plantation-owning family. I grew up with them.

Someone must take responsibility for the unmitigated failure, and I'm, apparently, the scapegoat.

What is good? All that heightens the feeling of power.

Shadows flicker behind the wooden door at the top of the stairs. A key turns and Captain Cates enters.

"Ever considered what our probable situation will be if we should be conquered in this war as I suspect we will be?" he asks, not waiting for a reply. "We'll be a humbled, down-trodden and disgraced people. Like slaves we'll do whatever our Northern masters demand. We'll lose our culture, our monuments, and repudiate our heroes."

What is evil? All that proceeds from weakness.

"Getting in a little insurance?" I ask.

"The country's divided… North, South… black… white… Americans slaughtering Americans with unequaled savagery. What I do or don't, hardly matters a damn."

I nod, finding myself in total agreement. "Shaky concepts like *nation* and *race* prevents the individual from finding a higher self."

"I've heard rumors about you Gray. Your men carried out that train attack in Missouri not a few months back. A massacre I'm told. Just a handful Union soldiers on leave after the battle around Atlanta, but you and your men killed everyone… all the passengers."

"Killing the enemy means winning the war and going home. I kill as many as I can, whenever and wherever I can."

"Men, women and children."

"I figure killing the young is doing them a mighty big favor. Quickly saving them the pain of living through this life."

"Then we're hardly any different?" Cates wonders, failing to grasp how different we really are.

"I did a little asking around after I got back," I confess. He leans in closer to the bars; parallel shadows undulate his face. "Word is you've run up a stack of gambling debts and there's a foreclosure notice out on your family plantation. Best thing for you would be for the North to win, assuming you had a little good-will on hand. You're not the kind to help the Union for political reasons.... only for money."

"Difficult to prove."

"Sure, so I followed you. Saw you meeting a man. Handed you an envelope none too discreetly... Union spy most likely... and the envelope contained money I'd wager..."

"Perhaps you should have gone to Humphries with your story, but who'd believe Ezra, killer, and convicted traitor?"

What's happiness then? The feeling of power increasing.

"You know what they call Humphries back at HQ? The mushroom. 'Cause we keep him totally in the dark."

"Another difference with us," I say in a dead voice. "I'm not stupid."

"You're the one in the cell," Cates smirks.

"Then try the door."

Hesitantly, Cates reaches down and pokes at the handle. The cell door creaks open a few inches. "It's unlocked," he stammers.

"All doors unlock... if you push hard enough."

Silence for a while, then Cates laughs.

"Are you getting this Colonel?" I ask.

The door of a darkened cell at the end of the block opens. Colonel Humphries exits. "Affirmative Ezra, *the mushroom* heard it all."

Taking slow, solid steps he crosses to the captain.

"We rounded up that spy you met with Cornelius. Thing is I still couldn't believe it. I trusted you like a son. Even so, I too suspected leaks coming from high-command. I quickly narrowed it down to my office and knew that only meant one person. Ezra here offered to play out this charade and entice a confession."

Cates lifts his arms away from his body, as if in surrender, but from my low angle I glimpse silver in his palm. Humphries is slow on the draw. A shot from a single barreled *Derringer* rings out and Humphries crumples. Cates kicks the door back into the cell, hitting me in the face, and makes a run for it.

I take back what I said. I'll be happy to see this one swing.

1875. Making my way out of Bodie towards the Mexican border. Little more than a mile from the city limits I realize I'm being followed. Nothing obvious. Pin pricks on my neck. If you're a hunter, you soon realize when you're being hunted. They don't give themselves away by sloppiness. I consider laying an ambush, but it's such a nice day for a ride, and if all they're doing is following, then I figure why not let them… relax and enjoy the scenery?

If it's Cate's men, we'll meet soon enough.

How many times do you have to kill a man, I wonder? There's a grand irony at work that the job falls back to me. Captain Cates caused the death of many men under my command, lives I was responsible for, but the truth is I'd don't so much care about that. Some men just deserve a lot of killing. They scream out for it. Beg for it. Beg for the Grim Reaper to come and take them away.

Well, here I am.

I barely make it onto the moving train. Pushing through the bodies scattered in aisles on the carriages, I pick up a discarded revolver and check the chamber. Whoever it belonged to never got off a shot. Hysterical cries from survivors. Yeah, this is grief. A woman sobbing, draped across a husband. A desperate longing for the near-past. The knowledge that the future holds little in the way of delight. I almost put a shot into her head from behind, but I lack time and bullets.

It takes a period to get forward. Time for Cates to do his work. Rivers of blood winding left and right with every step. A whole lot of death to sift through. A whole heck of pain to walk through.

In that time Cates has also slaughtered the driver.

The fight between us, brutal, to the death—or so I think. The train enters a bridge over a ravine. I take my shot. A shovel of burning coal thrown into Cates face pitches him through the train door. I believe he falls to his death.

Nightfall. Metamorphosis… a sleepy little border town across the Rio Grande. Dusty hole. A room on the outskirts. A place to rest my head. Red sand cakes boardwalks… boots crunch grit. Men are gonna get killed here today, and I'm gonna kill 'em.

Creaking on the landing and my door explodes. Too eager… they should have waited some… till I might be asleep at least. I take out the first through the shattered frame of the door with my Winchester. A bullet through the wall and another cries out. Out onto the landing I kill a third. Seconds have passed. *The* Gunfight *at the* O.K. Corral was a 30-second shootout. Takes no time at all to kill men. Behind me, another gets off a shot, splintering railing. As I whirl to face him, his chest's torn open. Split seconds later the sound of the blast reaches me.

Four men lie dead as a thin figure advances up the stairs.

"Getting slow, huh?" A woman's voice. Dressed as a cowboy, she takes off her hat revealing a long spray of ink-black hair.

"Hmmp. I was getting to him," I mutter.

Ebony eyes set amid burnished mahogany skin.

"You've been following me since Texas," I observe.

"Just as well for you."

"Who are you?"

"My name is unpronounceable to you, but you can call me Ashwood."

"What do you want?"

"I'm a bounty-hunter. Same as you."

"The Captain?"

"Yes…. his men, I suppose? Cates is mine by the way."

"Gonna have to get in line."

"A lot of dead men..." The young woman pauses thoughtfully to admire our handiwork.

"You like killing?" I ask.

"Sure," she nods. "Who doesn't?"

"There's a certain right we have to deprive a man of life. Shall we…"

"Dispose of the bodies?" she cuts me off. "I quite like them where they are."

A flask. Ashwood drinks from it.

"Want some?"

Whiskey. My other addiction.

"I got some glasses inside the room."

Blood stained wood; stepping over bodies.

"When I masturbate," she begins, staring at the ground. "I can only get off thinking about killing people. Stabbing them mostly. Stabbing them, till I'm covered in blood."

A hand slides down her jeans, she touches herself in front of me. Forgetting herself. Unable to stop. At the table she pours two drinks. Hands me one with her finger deep in the amber liquid. I examine her appearance. Peaked eyebrows. Hard, dark nipples through a thin white shirt.

"Cherokee?" I ask.

"Some. My mother married a white farmer."

Noting my gaze, she slips off her shirt. A trail of dark hair runs down her belly disappearing into blackness in her jeans. There's a scar on her shoulder. An old wound. Bullet if I'm not mistaken.

Standing in the doorframe, the pool of blood beneath her feet is hardening, congealing into something permanent.

Drinking, we drift in time to the bed.

"Don't be gentle. Give orders," she says.

My hands slide through thick matted hair, looking into shark-like eyes; bestial and transformative.

"Hit me," she says. "Hit me hard."

I slap her face. Harder and harder. Till more blood paints walls. A europium. Descending into Hades. The drink sits on a barstool. Out of focus, it falls. Her laughing, bleeding face purrs.

Naked, young, perfect skin, she stands over me. Opening herself; her cunt wide, pink and wet, I am taken inside. Back to the beginning. Or the future.

Then I am fallen to Earth, surrounded by young and beautiful girls and boys. Drifting across the summer field of naked bodies, the air hangs languid with the scent of rotting hay. A black on a stage strangles strange mesmerising noises from a banjo… no, guitar. It lifts something in me; euphoria of the unknown.

Kelly says to me: “Isn’t he beautiful? Don’t you love Jimmy?”

Warm brown hair, she has paint dabbed across her nose in Cherokee patterns, a tie-dyed T-shirt knotted to reveal her belly. “You look really out of it Ezra. Did you drop some acid and not tell me?”

A puppet buoyed by the strings of the music, by the throngs of naked breasts, by the couples fucking in the mud, I scream at the top of my lungs: “Freedom!”

August 18, 1969.

“You really think you’re free while John Sinclair rots in prison?” Danny asks. Long haired proto-yippie, we have been friends since high school, when he was expelled for promoting atheism and attacking a teacher.

“What kind of future do you really want?” he asks me.

Staring down nuclear Armageddon, is this what our forbearers have bequeathed? Fuck peace and love. I just want to be left in peace to breathe.

“I’m going to move to San Francisco and become a painter,” Kelly says.

“What about you Ezra, what are you going to do?”

“I’m not going to die of old age,” I confess.

The Blackstone Club's a commune we set up in an old red brick warehouse in Haight-Ashbury. Kelly paints and Danny writes. People come and go. Danny will die at fifty-two by swallowing one hundred and fifty phenobarbital tablets with booze. Cancer will take Kelly in 1996.

Everything else is meaningless.

I see all their futures laid out ahead, as if pieces on a playing board, but I cannot see my own.

I'm dipping my head in and out of a bottle. A false sense of security. One evening I stagger home and Danny and Kelly are fucking on the couch. "What do you believe in?" she stops to ask.

"I'm a leftist. I believe in the reallocation of wealth and redistribution of power. I believe in universal health care for everyone. I believe in an end to corporate consumerism. I believe that it's obscene to have a single homeless person in the world. I believe in freedom."

Laughing at me, they go back to it. I sit in a corner and toss *Morrison Hotel* on the turntable.

My journey down the road of Rimbaud and Cobain disorders my senses. What am I missing from what I laboriously, so diligently desire to construct? A dull witted jailer rattles the keys of my cell. Shattered, stunted, the door swings open… and I cease to exist.

A drifter on the storm. Sun relentlessly bleaches a large compound in the Mexico desert. Sign reads: *The Blackstone*

Club. I ride in. When guards try to stop me I shoot them dead. One tries to run. I put a bullet in his back.

I jump down off my horse. Gunmen dot the veranda of the main building. Outnumbered twenty to one.

“My name is Ezra Gray,” I address the men inside the compound. “Many of you will know my reputation. I have come for the man known as El Capitán. I have no interest in the rest of you. You may all leave here unharmed. If you stay you will die. It doesn’t mean much to me either way. You have one minute to decide.”

Inside the building, some motion. Captain Cates moves out of the darkness, a twisted mask of scar tissue peers into the light. He orders his men to open fire, but they are having second thoughts. They *do* know my reputation. Paid killers, they have no real loyalty to El Capitán. To walk free is too tempting. One by one they leave the building, throw down their arms, and escape on horseback. Soon only Cates remains.

“Don’t give up, huh?” he calls.

“I hear there’s a new kind of racism emerging in society,” I tell him. “Lookism—the discrimination against people’s appearance to the detriment of their wellbeing. Ugliness it seems is no different from gender or race.”

“Well while I may no longer be endowed with your fine looks, I’m not rushing to get a lawyer. Though, it’s sure comforting to have my long-held suspicions confirmed—beautiful people have an easy time of it.”

Reaching into the darkness, he drags Ash to her feet. Beaten, a noose around her neck, he shelters behind her naked body.

“Tell your story girl. Tell what happened when your folks found me. Near dead… my face burned beyond recognition.”

"My… mother and father… tried to help…"

I can see where this is going.

Ashwood tells her story. Cates survives the fall into the ravine, discovered by a farmer and his family. His face burned, no one recognizes him. They nurse him back to health, but suspicious, begin asking questions in nearby towns. Cates knows it's a matter of time. He has to escape. Attempting to steal a gun, he's discovered by the wife and children. The farmer returns home to find his family shot—dead and dying in a pile. His youngest daughter, wounded, the sole survivor.

I tipped him in her family's direction.

"Risen from the ashes," Cates places a pistol barrel at her temple.

Yeah. Somewhat scarred.

"Seems like no one's here just for the bounty, not even the farmer's half-breed Injun daughter?"

"Ugly fucker. Ugly fucking fuck," Ashwood begins to chant. "Why, I saw better looking hogs drinkin' at Shit Stream. How'd you get to be so ugly? Did your cunt of a mother look as bad? D'ya break all the mirrors in your house?" Spitting blood, she continues to taunt Cates. "Cunt. Fucking ugly prick."

That's right. Look to me. Lose control. I'm the one the who caused your scars. I'm to blame.

He pushes his prisoner down on her knees to execute her—and I fire.

The bullet clips her and embeds itself in his gut. A slow death, if she'd let it be. Groaning Cates clutches his stomach to avoid it disinterring. Struggling to crawl away.

Wrestling the knife from the sheath on his belt, like a viper, she's upon him.

I walk a snail's pace.

Blood sand trails… burrowed by worms from the depths of hell. Bringing the knife down again and again, her skin's red; flecks daub her body. "Oh god, oh god."

Killing. Cumming. I can't hardly tell anymore. Hard to tell where he ends and she begins.

I have a vision of the future. Spinning, disintegrating, pieces scattering to infinity. I snatch back some of those fragments as they pierce the sky. White teeth smiling wide, a soy boy at a coffee house orders a soy latte in a desperate attempt to get pussy. Decrying toxic western masculinity, a third-wave feminist masturbates over the misogyny of Islam. Faux-cool clutches of hipster clones enjoy mediocre comfort in the sad embrace of conformity. *Don't fat shame me* cries an obese young woman ignoring the tell-tale twinges as fatty deposit plaques rupture in her heart's arteries, pitching her and thousands of other over-consumers into early oblivion. Freedom… just around the corner.

Los Alamos, New Mexico. Me? I keep moving. I keep my head down. An ex-wife or two, some children trail edges of my history. My mind forgets things. Everything is speeding up. Rushing through life. I'm born. For a while I'm a child. That doesn't last. My dad is a blue-collar worker, servicing trucks and other vehicles most of his short life. Avoid the dirt and grease, he says. I listen to my old dad. At twenty-two I'm a cowboy. Later, I join the local sheriff's department.

All well and good till a routine traffic stop goes bad, and some amphetamine-fueled fuck puts a bullet in my gut. I shoot some people and he shoots me. I prefer to be the killer. It makes a man think twice about his choices.

P.I. Chasing down deadbeat dads who haven't paid their child support in years, or solo-mums who've shot up loans on oxycodone. A nifty acronym for a bounty hunter. It pays the rent. It buys the whisky. Functioning. I keep thinking about that word. I order a black coffee. The second of the morning. I touch my black Stetson to the waitress who brings it over. A black T-shirt, jeans and boots complete the outfit. Outward appearance is very important, especially when you're falling apart inside. Especially when you're dealing with corporate clients like the jackass sitting in front of me.

Insurance guy hands me the folder and I flick through it, scanning the facts. Young man named John Bridge. Twenty-five years old. A fatal motorcycle incident and a claim filed by his wife under workplace injury.

"The claim goes back two years," he says checking his phone.

"Where's it been? Sitting on someone's desk?"

"Could be. Dunno, to be honest. The company wants you to check it out."

"Guy's on the way to work—you got yourself a workplace accident. What's your angle?"

"There are some questions—the claimant says she's the worker's wife, though his work colleagues didn't know her, and also the incident was almost two hundred miles from the workplace."

"Marriage certificate?"

“Report says we had a copy, but it must have got lost.”

“The usual fees, usual retainer.”

I pay and tip the waitress and she asks if I have *Facebook*?

Opportunist cashing in on death? I like to keep an open mind. Plastics factory on the outskirts of town. Plastics, their production and destruction contribute to global warming, they say. So too do fossil fuels. Digging from the Earth what should remain there.

Company management’s co-operative. They want it settled. Provide me details of John Bridge’s employment. Worked here three years. Reliable. No problems. Meager income. The wealthiest 1% of the world’s population owns more than half of the world’s wealth. Welcome to the land of I don’t give a fuck.

Insurance guy’s right. No one can remember the wife. It gets worse ‘cause down on the work floor I struggle to find anyone who remembers the kid himself.

“I think he used to work on the packaging line.”

“Don’t know him at all, sorry.”

“Dye-casting?”

I kick around the cafeteria a bit and finally find a few former colleagues who recognize the name and picture.

“John was quiet, y’know?”

“Kept to himself.”

“He just did his work. Didn’t bother no one.”

Quiet young family man. A no one. An everyone. An isolated life which does not scratch the surface of expected social interaction. Once we are dead we are not even memories. Bridge stayed at a caravan park during the working week. No education means options dwindle into nothingness. I think of an empty room… an empty bottle. I call the park, but the owner says it's changed hands, and he doesn't know Bridge, he doesn't have any old records, and he doesn't know where the former owner is. He does recall the former owner's name. I call everyone in the state phone book with that name. Finally, I get my man. He remembers the deceased.

"John'd stay at the park near the workplace during the week and travel back home to his wife in a remote no horse town at the weekend."

I drive into the middle of nowhere, but still can't find the wife. She isn't at any address I have, nor does she answer her phone. Time's passed. Stopping for petrol I notice my image on a security camera screen. Tracked and watched at every turn; freedom a tentative promise. Paying the cashier, I ask in passing if he knows her? He gives me directions to a house.

Opening the door, Rebecca Bridge nods emotionlessly when I explain the purpose of my visit. Part-Cherokee, attractive but for sad eyes; she invites me in. Photographs dot the small cell-like room; souvenirs from distant places hint domesticity.

"I miss John still," she says. "I didn't expect to be a widow so young. The money will help. How long do you think it will be before I get the money?"

I take a look around the shack and shrug.

"How do you get by?"

Rebecca sighs. “John had to travel. He died on the way to work on a Monday morning. There’s no work here and we couldn’t afford to move to the city. Rent’s too high.”

Property’s freedom. Not having to be fucked around on the whim of banks or landlords. Digital short-term rentals and foreign buyers drive up prices; wage and rent slavery flourishes. Welcome to disruptive innovation, the epitome of the American scream.

“Normally he’d go to the caravan on a Sunday night but that weekend was our wedding anniversary. He stayed Sunday night and travelled Monday, early in the morning, ran off the road. My fault.”

“Reckon we all have a day out there that’ll be our last,” I say. “Not much that can be done.”

“I work as a cam-girl for a club in Albuquerque. I work there two nights, then come home.”

There’s something in her black eyes I cannot read. Lust and loneliness rush in.

“I like you,” she says. “If you want I can make your trip out here worthwhile? If you could tell the insurance company what they want to hear.”

I close my eyes and imagine.

“My people have a story,” the young woman says. “We are told that toward the end of the world, the Spider Woman will come and she will weave a web across the landscape. Everywhere you go you will see it. That’s how we’ll know that this world is coming to an end, when we see her web everywhere.”

A chill creases my spine.

“I believe I have seen her web,” I say. “I see it every day.”

I call my client and let them know the story checks out. The voice on the phonc sounds vaguely disappointed. Dogs eat dogs eat dogs.

Hanging out for a drink I reach into the glove compartment and take out a bottle of Jack Daniels. A few swigs and I see the future. Glint of silver across my eyes. I miss the turn-off to the highway back to Los Alamos, shrug and drive further into the borderlands. Rust dust swirls ahead in a limitless splintered cloud, dancing patterns made and remade on cosmic whim. Hand slides to my belt and I take out the .38 revolver. Tough, reliable, a very rough pull. Chains rattle on my wrists.

Bridge falls across a divide. Cracks in our nation as we slip into insanity. The web slivers across the landscape as I stare deep into the gaping hole in the United States of America. Stifling dullards tripping over ignorance. Inept leadership. Fake news left and right. Religious fundamentalism. Constant outrage. An uneducated populace. Identity politics. Groupthink. Idolizing fools. Bipartisanship. Virtue signaling. Political correctness. An unbigoted wave lays waste to humanity. Vast tribal groups disinterred. Proteinaceous spider silk extrudes from spinnerets. Rudderless… near… the horn of the dark age sounds.

The bottle of whiskey in my hand is the holy grail. And I know exactly what to do with it.

Next to the compound there's a water tower where shivering and shaking Ashwood gets herself cleaned up. The dead rest.

Too bad about the living.

10

WILD HONEY

The town begins to fall asleep. Darkness virtually meaningless to me; life is a series of prematurely dusk blurred images. I cannot sleep. Instead, I press/stab sharp pencil into paper, leaving small indentations that I can trace and re-read later.

When I was ten, I decided to be a writer and craft sadness into words. For grief defines us: our mother, myself, and of course Mila.

Dot marks pause on paper.

There are patterns everywhere.

Empty bottles of wine on a small glass table. Our mother is still not awake. Mila looks at the clock on a wall of faded wallpaper. Patterns within patterns. Past mid-day. Mila says she understands our mother's loneliness. Deep scars mark thin pale wrists.

"She's killing herself slowly," I reply.

"Yes," Mila whispers.

"What can we do?"

"Escape."

Just shy of her twenty-first birthday escape seems all the more possible for Mila.

Mila has met someone.

"He lives in a nearby Khrushchyovka. I would like you to meet him. His name is Lev."

"Of course."

Mila bites her nails. "I have felt so very alone and undeserving of human affection."

"I hope you will be happy," I say. *Oh no,* I think. *Don't be obsessive, I want to say. Don't slash your wrists over this one,* I want to add.

Our mother fails to wake this day—a persistent tranquilized state that no matter how much I try—I'm unable to rouse her. Mila leaves to spend time with her boyfriend. I'm left alone considering whether to call a doctor—when finally, our mother wakes.

"I've never felt better," she says brightly.

A giant meteor shower streaks across central Ukraine lighting up the night sky. A few months ago. Mila describes it to me as a series of fiery lights coming to earth. The excited locals call it *Bilyy Podiya*—the White Event. It's a sleepy town where little happens. Perhaps a blessing in a country being slowly torn apart.

A cold blue autumn morning machine-guns light through the skeletal trees. Merged into stick taps, I pick up a low-level buzzing frequency. A cursed family—that was how I hear people refer to us. Three broken people. The disabled child—the last in a long line of brokenness. My hearing is better than fine, thank you. The bees are nearby. I take small pride picking objects amidst the murk. The latticed bark on the tree trunk where the bees gather. Discarded soda bottle. Movement. An animal. Cat or squirrel? Too far away. I give up. My father kept bees. He would tell me random bee facts. Like during colder seasons, worker bees can live for nine months. But in the summer, they rarely last longer than six weeks—they literally work themselves to death. He worked at the uranium mine and died in a tunnel collapse. Trekking slowly across my path the animal returns. I smile momentarily as I recognize a black cat. The Soviet-era Khrushchyovkas that dot the landscape are hive-like.

Tuesday and Thursday mornings I make my way to the apartment of Mr. Marakov, a retired school teacher. He can be brisk; in my mother's era he had a reputation for rewarding wrong answers by wrapping a student's knuckles with a ruler. I knock without an answer.

"Mr. Marakov?"

Boxes hug the walls of a long narrow hallway which leads to the living room. Communist-designed furniture and décor. An old man sits in a couch chair. His head back and his mouth open.

"Asleep?"

Outside, there's general lethargy in the air, beyond the cold empty expressions of people going about their solitary lives, beyond the drunks passed out from alcohol-poisoning mid-afternoon. Inside, I walk down supermarket rows devoid of life.

"Hurry up," calls the shopkeeper. "We're closing soon."

"It's two in the afternoon," I protest.

"We're closing early."

The town is slowly going to sleep.

Mila sits on my bed in darkness while we play the music of John Lennon. Echoes of the past, when we were both children, but Mila's moving away from me.

"He is a beautiful man. He is the one I will stay with."

Lev. She's talking again about Lev. "He came from the East, he and his family and colleagues. They came to work in the mine. He is a scientist. He does some high-level job. Something about geo-mechanics. Sometimes he explains it to me but I don't understand everything. He makes me feel so good. Not just sex, but everything. I feel so good around him. Can there really be one important person for us Kateryna? I think if there is Lev is mine."

"It's so very hard to be happy. I hope that you can be happy with this person Mila."

"I am so very sensitive. I cannot live like other people: alone. I want you to meet him, but not mother. I don't want him to see her. I want to be better than her. Love, is transformative; we seek it to change into something else. Something we may like."

"We should go to bed," I tell her. "You look sleepy."

When we do Mila does not wake for six days.

The sleeping sickness that comes to the town strikes down young and old. The afflicted succumb suddenly—at work in mid-conversation, in the street—lowered flags truncated upon themselves. I collect the stories. The business man who passes out driving mid phone call, narrowly missing a child on a bike. The mayor who face-plants cabbage borshch. The coma state can last several days.

Upon waking some experience momentary euphoria, others memory loss and hallucinations. Encephalitis lethargica, the sleeping sickness of the 1920s is quickly eliminated as a possible cause, as is African trypanosomiasis. Mass hysteria is considered.

"I am really fine," Mila insists. "The best I have ever felt."

The most popular idea is that it's related to the nearby uranium mine, yet scientists from the Institute of Radiation Medicine and Ecology are dispatched to measure radon levels, to test soil and ground water, and they find nothing.

There's another theory: the Russians.

Mila's euphoria can't last. A strange incident occurs in the hospital shortly before she's released. Mila's crying and when I approach the room, I hear a man's voice respond. He speaks in a clipped Russian accent. Lev is Russian? His speaking style is strange, as if he learned language from an old recording.

"I'm sorry, I didn't mean it to end like this."

"Where will you go?"

"Siberia. Away from people."

Mila is sobbing and incoherent. I move closer, straining to hear more clearly. The man replies that it will not be the same. No, that he will not be the same. He says more things I do not understand. I hear some words which sound like: *Queen mandibular pheromone.* He talks of formulas and acid. Trying to explain something to her. He's a scientist, and it goes over my head and Mila's too. All she cares about is Lev is leaving.

My own sleep remains troubled. I wake several times a night, go to the toilet and return for more tossing and turning. One night I rouse as the front door closes.

"Mila?"

I follow threading my way easily through the night. Outside the white blur of Mila's night dress moves towards Lev's building. It's icy. Tonight's seen the first winter snow fall.

"Mila!"

Inside the stairwell there's strange buzzing… I grab Mila's arms, and she wakes—eyes wide open.

"Mila! You're sleepwalking!"

"Leave me…" Her hands reach out in reflex.

The building's long been in disrepair. An innocent push. A missing step that I cannot see. Two flights. I land on the ground with a force that takes the air from my chest and I feel something inside crack. Blood upon my lips.

Footsteps rushing to me. Mila's calling my name, and the man's voice: "It will be okay."

My vision's blurred, mostly darkness, but the glow above transfixes me as Lev's hand touches my chest. Warmth across me and I can breathe again. Something else. A trust in his words. Yes, everything will be okay. The hands, strong but gentle hands moving higher.

Then my vision clears.

I see my sister for the first time. I see the man who holds me. Honey drips from catacomb walls where similar creatures hang bat-like in darkness. Mila was right. He's beautiful.

"It's really okay," Mila says.

Thoughts spiral, the fever-pitch buzzing, and finally... I sleep… and in the dream my father comes to me.

"What do you know about bee pheromones?" I ask him.

"Well, bees give off pheromones for different reasons. Most create harmony within the hive. Some are for mating, or orientation, others produce calming effects to stop individuals fighting. Why do you ask?"

"Why can people not do the same?"

The lamp glows hypnotically by the bed.

I think of Mila and want to write of her deep love of a man from a different place, but nothing comes and I stare remotely at a handful of written words on a page. I think about the note she left behind. The night she walked out into snow. A few weeks after Lev's departure. I kept it in my drawer and reach for it. Folding back the paper I read her words.

They never found her and I don't think they ever will. In my stories Mila is always safe in another place—in Siberia with a man who is not the same. A man I believe will take care of her. A man who can in all likelihood take care of anything. My Mila, the warmth and love she longed for, that humans denied her, at last hers, wild and transformed.

11

COLD OPHELIA

The lake water laps against the bank. Something welcoming to its softness, promise, whisper. Fragile scents of lilies and driftwood. My feet sink into earth, mud pressing through toes like coruscating watercolors onto a palette. High above, sparrows nest in weeping willows. Tilting my head, I listen to their animated twitter. As a child, I loved the sound of birds.

I live, adept at treading water. Not as a native aquatic dweller might, furnished with nature's gills, easily pushing life-giving oxygen through veins, but alone, struggling to breathe with a vastness of water on all sides.

Diving towards the drab wooden building, I allow my mind to uncoil, letting all the distant sounds submerge me: a beauty and a relaxant quality to their language. For days I float along tranquil currents, decayed roses falling, a soft pitter-patter as clouds daub grey sky. I have learned to surround myself with methods to stay afloat. Voices are passing driftwood. Should I cling to one? And if I do, where precisely will it take me?

Puddles in potholes dot the carpark.

A trickle. A sound. It's raining upon the ocean tonight. It's not time. Rising. I burst the surface surrounded by waves and hear the sounds of driftwood bobbing, clanking into each other, wooden clogs on a neoprene floor.

Sparkling and shining, water cascades from a bathroom tap into porcelain. A child-woman stares at a basin in delight.

"You haven't seen her before?" An oaky hollow sound reverberates in the man's voice.

"Autistic?" I ask.

From the corridor I look through a sheet of glass, catching the reflection of strangers discussing the teenager's past and future; a girl who does not hear us, nor even register our presence. For her, there's only water.

"Yeah, close to a worst-case scenario."

I continue to watch the girl in the next room with fascination; red-haired, pale, distant, cut off from human contact, absorbed in her own world. Rain patters against exterior windows.

"She doesn't speak—but she can understand language. She can sign. Some nurses insist they've heard her say stuff but I'm doubtful," Phil replies in monotone. A staff psychiatrist; stiff, young, retaining no trace of boyhood enthusiasm for life. At times I imagine breaking him out of his cocoon, though have some idea of what that might involve.

"How old is she?"

"Sixteen. She's pretty much spent her whole life in institutions like this."

Lake Alice, a rural psychiatric facility named after the nearby lake. The hospital officially opened in August 1950, is self-sufficient, with its own farm, workshop, bakery, laundry, swimming pools, glasshouses, and vegetable gardens. The isolation mirrors the type of patients; long stay chronic cases who rarely receive visitors.

"When's the last time someone reviewed her case?" I ask, pressing my face to the glass. "I remember reading recently about new therapies in a journal. There are a couple of experimental new drugs."

"At this stage of her life it's probably a little too little, too late. Let it go Jane. Come on, the patient you've come to see's down in the ward."

"And waste all those years of university and hard work? Can't you do something? Maybe get me assigned to her?" Affecting emotion, a dry smile cuts across my face.

"Well, I dunno... maybe if you agreed to dinner this time?"

I turn and give him a *don't go there again* look.

"Phil, you know my situation. Don't make things worse for me."

"Sorry." He raises his hands in surrender. "I'll do what I can."

Outside the sun's come out; heat sucks up shrinking puddles. Steam evaporates and I with it.

Frost icy upon hard earth. Holly Reed sits barefoot on a bench in the hospital grounds. Never feeling the cold, at least never complaining. Absorbed in squiggles and lines on the sketch-pad in front of her, she doesn't respond. When I raise her head and place her face between my hands to achieve eye contact,

Holly focuses on a spot in the middle of my forehead. As I move her head upwards to get her to meet my eyes, she lifts her gaze to my forehead again.

I gather twigs and flowers from a nearby garden. “There’s rosemary, that’s for remembrance. Pray you, love, remember. And there are pansies, for your thoughts.”

Holly ignores the bouquet and turns back to sketching.

Reading Holly’s file provides a few interesting details. Holly had always been a sketcher, but the drawings, remarkably detailed, don’t fit the usual stages of childhood development. She drew in perspective at age three, something most children fail to achieve until adolescence. I’ve seen these splinter skills or *islets of ability* previously in autistic children.

“I read about your mum Holly, about how she gave you up when you were five. Parents don’t always do the right thing.” I lean over the younger girl’s shoulder. “They tell me you draw only flowers and scenery. Would you like to come for a walk? We can find something new for you to draw?” I reach out and take Holly’s hand. The girl displays no reaction. She does not willingly rise to her feet, but neither does she fight it.

Occasionally Holly pauses to touch or smell leaves, and in isolated moments, looks briefly at, and then past me. It makes me an unimportant part of her world. Earlier, I run a test. I tell Holly a story describing a child called Sally who puts her toy away in a basket and then goes out of the room. But while she’s away, another girl, Annie, moves it to her box. When asked where Sally, on her return, thinks the toy is, Holly points that Sally thinks it was in Annie’s box—where it *really* is—rather than the basket where Sally would have *thought* it is.

In a nearby field, a group of hospital staff and patients play soccer. One man kicks a ball, and it lands close to Holly's feet. I watch as Holly takes a step, reaches to pick up the ball, and holds it up to her face. She sniffs the object suspiciously, and as the ball's owner rushes up to us, drops it neatly into his expectant hands.

"Do you mind throwing us the ball again?" I ask. The man nods happily, but when I turn around, Holly's gone. Spotting the glint of sun on water, she's off running—down to the lake at breakneck pace.

"No Holly!" I call, rushing after her. But Holly has a good head-start; reaching the edge she doesn't stop, but keeps on running down the bank, slipping into the muddy water below. I follow her in without hesitation. I grab hold of one of the girl's wrists, realizing suddenly there's no danger. Holly stops splashing and looks at me.

"When you was three mother me bought a small black and white kitten."

"What? You can talk—you can talk!" I cry. "Holly, it's true!"

"You don't understand people. You never know what they are going to do next."

The phone call triggers me a little.

"It's your father's birthday. You could at least wish him a nice day. It's only polite."

"Don't ask me to talk to him."

"You have to let things go Jane. Hanging onto the past will do your head in."

Leather straps coil around my head. My wrists are tied to the gurney. A place like Lake Alice. Sheets of electrical current slash through my body. Convulsing with the rhythmic shaking of a seizure. My mind is splintering, fragments strewn in all directions. That's what you get for a suicide attempt and being female in 1967. Lucky I suppose. Rosemary Kennedy suffered a knife through the brain for mood swings.

A waterfall of emotions ease to a trickle. Numb, I tread off-white corridors decked in zombies. After a half dozen treatments, a doctor tells me I'm cured. I can rejoin society again. Shrugging, I thank him. I don't feel cured. I feel at rock bottom. Is this what it means to be *normal*? I rejoin my course of study, finding purpose and finally reaching comfortable coexistence with my suicidality.

Holly sits in her room in front of the TV playing the same video tape of *Punch and Judy* over and over, showing great delight when characters trip, or fall, or hurt each other.

Judy: Where is the child?
Punch: Gone, gone to sleep.
Judy: What have you done with the child, I say.
Punch: Gone to sleep, I say.
Judy: What have you done with it!

Passing the door, I pause a moment to peer inside—before continuing walking with Phil, awkwardly and with pain.

"There's a school, for autistic children, in Wellington. They're willing to take her," Phil says. "The care they provide is based on the Doucecrift School approach—which take the view we are all born autistic, although most of us quickly grow out of it. The teachers there believe it's their job to find the trigger that will enable autistic children to find meaning in a world that is, to them, frightening, incomprehensible and frustrating."

Reaching the visitors room, we sit in the bench chairs. His eyes I note, linger too long on my face. *(The bruise, perhaps?)*

"But there's a problem," he says. "She's pregnant."

"What? How did that even happen? That girl's practically catatonic."

"Beats me... an orderly, a doctor, another patient... we're looking into it. The school won't take her until the baby's born. If the child's normal it'll be adopted out, if not it's going straight into care. That's the best we can offer."

My eyes catch Phil's, and he takes it as an opening to reach and touch my cheek. Not even a flinch. Instead, my eyes fix darkly into space. He runs his hand through my hair letting it fall in a shroud over my face.

"Keep your head above water," he says.

I walk into the lake. Gentle reeds brush against my legs. A breeze caresses my back and I pause waist deep in water. Lake tides wash my white dress till it clings like glad-wrap. I stare at the water for a long time.

Tumultuous storms are ever present in the deep. Nowhere to hide, nowhere to go but down. Sinking beneath the surface I explore a world of darkness, infinite cavernous rocks, revealed by touch rather than sight or sound. Down and deeper to a landscape devoid of all life. Here is the place everything ends. Plastic. Debris. Decaying plant life and the rotting corpses of the once-alive. The water no longer moves. A thick film of compost blankets everything and with it comes the stagnant, pungent stench of decay. Nothing could live down here in this murk, surely… and yet, even here on the floor, where the tides of the ocean have all but extinguished, something moves.

Then… to my left, fingers, tentatively touch mine. A hand, not clasped in mine. *Holly.* I don't dare look. Something beneath the water brushes my leg. The caress of extremities. A woman's hand breaks the surface. Then another. They are everywhere. The lake is a water garden of female digits, growing, flourishing in the blue-green. Generation upon generation of hands. A poet puts rocks in her coat pockets and walks into the river Ouse. In a London home, a writer smells the first hint of gas from the open oven door. An actress attempts suicide on numerous anniversaries of her child's death, eventually succeeding August 30, 1979. A 29-year-old woman who wants to be married and who isn't, shoots herself live on television. Beautiful suicides. Young women bullied into oblivion. An unbroken line back to Cleopatra.

Flocculent clouds form and reform, finally settling on an indistinct, alien shape.

The pull of the ocean floor.

Todd's late again and I'm prepared. A briefcase of papers from work pepper the solid wooden restaurant table. Clearing room for the impending meal I accidently brush correspondence onto the floor. A card covered in hand-drawn hearts lands face up. I sigh and reach down, but it's Todd's hand that picks it up.

Pin-pricks in my arm.

"Who's that from?" he asks, tossing the card back onto the table. "Another one of them?"

I've been with this man for five years. We've survived all kinds of difficulties that would've broken most other couples up years ago. He was there for me. He is there for me.

"It was one of my patients," I confess.

He encourages me.

"What did he want?"

He understands a breakdown.

"Uummm..."

"Shit—he wanted you to go out with him, didn't he? What do you do to them?" he asks, but what he really means is: *What do you do to encourage them?*

I cannot blame him, his questions, his jealousy.

"Nothing!" I cry, always unprepared for the inevitable questioning.

"You must do something to lead them on—because let's face it—you're just not that pretty."

I look down at the wooden table-top and imagine it floating away downstream. The food arrives and Todd begins to eat in silence. I murmur an excuse. In a chunky wood-panel bathroom, I stare into the mirror and run water in the basin.

"Holly has a problem with syntax: the rules of grammar which allow us to combine words in understandable phrases, and the deixis of speech—those words that have shifting meaning—

words like *here* and *now*, *now* and *then* and *you* and *I*. She's like a lot of children with autism—she refers to herself by her first name or says you when she means I," I exhale as the sound of my voice fades, and Todd's wrinkled brow softens. "It's not like a complete breakthrough or anything—she's clammed up and hasn't spoken since, but that there was a reaction is amazing."

"Yeah, wonderful. So long as she doesn't fall in love with you too. So long as you don't want to bring her home or anything…?"

I regard him cautiously. Realization dawns, and he doesn't bother to hide his disdain. "You've got to be kidding. You've got to be out of your mind!"

I want him to share in my world, but try as I might, everything's always on his terms. It seems he will forever shut me out, break my will, win.

"It's only for a couple of weeks—just to get her out of that hospital—ECT is still performed there on patients—it's not the right environment for her. It's just until I can find a better place in residential care," I plead, grabbing his arm.

"Do you realize what you're saying? By your own admission, the girl's fucking crazy!"

"Don't say that! You're so selfish Todd—can't you for once think of someone else!"

He throws me roughly off, raising his hand, palm upturned in a swift jerky motion. As his flexed fingers pause in mid-air, my heart quickens. There's silence for an eternity, before his hand drops, impotently to his side. I slink to the wall.

"How could you... how could you even think of that... after you know what I went through with my father... how could you?"

"I'm sorry baby, I'm sorry. I wouldn't have... you know..."

"Don't call me baby ever again—don't."

"Come here," Todd says in an unreadable voice. At first his move is apologetic, tender even, stroking my hand; then he grabs me roughly by the arm and drags me kicking into the bedroom. My screams do not stop him. Love is not all hearts and flowers.

Holly's hand clutches mine. She will not let go until I tell her everything.

"I know—or I suspect, or I dread—that my legs will exhaust and I will slip beneath the surface, but I don't want it to be now," I admit.

Holly stares at the water for a long time. Finally, she concludes:

"You'll always have the water."

"I fear I may want to die forever."

"That's just how it is."

12

WALL OF DEATH

Been in some bad situations. Some bad places. I've had bad things done to me and done bad things to others. I don't want to go into them. It's not necessary. Use your imagination.

It wasn't always this way. Once I was the same as anyone else. It seems to me that I was set on this course to self-destruction long ago.

Ten years ago.

The beating old man Priddy gives me is a bad as any I've had. I'm eighteen and make the mistake of standing up to him. I should have known better. Should have known my place.

It's when Mike, the sheriff's deputy, becomes involved that I feel my ribs break and begin coughing blood.

"That's for touching my daughter you piece of shit!" The old man's call accompanies a kick which takes the rest of breath from my lungs.

As I writhe on the ground, I hear Mike telling him that's enough—that he and the boys will take care of me. I feel grateful to Mike for that. I want to thank him. Rape of a minor—the old man and his daughter won't see me inside of ten years, or so Mike says.

Juliana comes to the door and I can hear her screaming. I can hear her screaming. Ten years.

The car swallows the road. Blurred desert terrain of rolling hills and tumbleweed. I'm in the middle of nowhere, but I'm going somewhere. Yeah, I'm going home.

They say that you shouldn't go back—that you should only go forward, but I think you have to revisit the past at some point in order to get on with the future. I read that somewhere. I did a lot of reading in prison. Educated myself—hadn't had a lot of time for books before. But time is all you have in prison.

It's not a good environment for an eighteen-year-old kid from small-town USA... hell on earth... you either fight or fuck... I don't want to go into it...

I recognize the gas station/bar/diner which passes for civilization in these parts. It's the first of my old haunts. I know now I don't have far to go.

Thirst and hunger draws me in. Mostly thirst for numbness.

"Bourbon," I order.

I lay it down and order another. Another.

"You from around here pal?" the barman asks after a while. He tells me I seem kind of familiar, which makes me smile.

“Looking for a girl,” I say. “Juliana Priddy. You know her?”

“You wanna stay clear of that one. She’s bad news. Crazy they say. Old man Priddy is too. There’re bad things gone on in that family. You ain’t kin, are you?”

“Let’s say I owe them something.”

I light a match, touch it to the edge of a cigarette and watch the smoke drift away.

Ten years ago. Or longer. Shit, I can’t even remember now. A field of grass in summer. We’re passing the smoke from a joint between each other’s lips. Juliana and I.

She’s very stoned and lies back, placing her hand on her breast. Her eyes are dark and glistening, chin pointed, cascades of black hair tossed back over her bare shoulders. She has a series of freckles that dot her face almost randomly. Sometimes she tries to cover them up with make-up, but today her face is clear, and I start to count her freckles. When you’re in love with someone, really in love, you don’t look at all their perfect attributes, but their faults, and the faults are suddenly all the more endearing. You fall in love with their imperfections.

“I fuckin’ love drugs, don’t you?” she says. It’s not so much a question as a statement.

“Sure.”

“Have you ever tried coke?” she asks me, sitting back up, hugging her knees. “This cleaner salesman that passed through here six months ago gave me some. All he wanted was a blow job in return.”

“And you did it?”

"Sure. What the hell—I didn't swallow or anything. You know what's best about drugs? When I take them all the things that make me feel bad and miserable disappear. It's the only time I'm ever happy."

She lifts up her dress and I lie beside her rubbing her stomach, smelling her gentle sweetness. Even then, though we're both unaware, there's a child growing inside her.

She slips out of her dress and I take down my jeans. Her arms make me crazy. Inside her I'm complete.

Intense eyes beneath me, gaze up. "I enjoy this with you," she murmurs.

"Me too."

"I enjoy it with you. Not like when father makes me have sex with him."

"What?"

I loved her... or at least my eighteen-year-old self did, and now I'm retarded to that age—tied inexplicably to that girl. My first love and my last.

There's one more stop I have to make before entering the town. It's on the outskirts and abandoned like so much in this place of my childhood.

The old motorcycle track. My father helped build it back in the old days when circuses were still touring through this area. Hell, there was so little to do here.

My old man used to be a motorcycle rider in the old days. He used to ride the wall of death. I remember childhood grease-splattered afternoons in the sun when he used to take me out on the back. He taught me everything he knew. I was proud of him, my old man.

I'd like to do that again. One last ride on the wall of death.

This town's hardly changed at all. If anything it's grown more depressed and confining. The people glance suspiciously from sidewalks as I drive slowly by. They don't like strangers here.

Soon enough word will spread to Sheriff Mike. I don't have much time.

The house is run down, neglected—a veritable rickety shack on the verge of collapse. Grass sprouts sporadically in the yard, but mostly there's just dust. Power lines droop, sadly neglected overhead on narrow wooden poles. The term *poor white trash* springs to mind.

It's going to happen.

Nervous for some reason, nauseous even, and it's a comfort because I haven't felt anything in a long time. I run my hands through my hair and slip on a pair of Ray-Bans, checking the result in the rear-view mirror. Looks are very important.

The gun is a .45 automatic. It weighs heavy in my hands. It's been ten years. I wonder what she looks like?

Outside.

There's a little girl in the gutter.

"Hi, do you live here," I ask exiting the car.

"Yeah—what's it to you?" she replies without looking up. Her appearance matches exactly her angry tone. Sandy blond hair and torn clothes, torn heart.

"Is Juliana here still?"

"Yeah, she's my mother."

"And your grandfather?"

"Don't know where he is. Don't care either."

I'm beginning to like this child. "What's your name?"

"Heather."

"That's a nice name Heather. My mother's name was Heather. Would you like to go on a trip Heather?"

"Where?"

"Anywhere you like. It's your choice."

"Okay."

"Wait here," I tell her.

Boxes and beer cans piled up to windows. Dirt or mud, or who knows what on the floor. Dishes unwashed in the sink.

Walking disinterested through the squalor, I reach her room. The door is closed. "Juliana?"

A pause and I open it.

Inside there's a woman lying prone on the bed. She groans at the sound of my voice and I move closer. She's wearing—what are those things called—it's been so long, a slip? A petticoat?

Whatever. It's sheer and made from silk. I'm unable to resist the temptation to touch those white shoulders, and she rolls her head towards me. I think of each individual strand of her hair, and shake her lightly, and then more roughly. She's not asleep. Drugged. Has she done this to herself, or has he done it to her?

Her face is reddened and the skin blotchy around the eyes. She has tiny bruises all over her body. "Shit what's he done to you?"

I lift her up, taking her small weight easy in my arms. She's cold to the touch as I carry her out through the living room. All I'm thinking about is getting her away from this.

It's as I come into the sun I receive the blow across the back of my head and everything spins. I hear the voice.

"You've got to be crazy kid, to come back here..."

Juliana rolls away and the gun's too far for me to reach. The old man hits me again with the iron bar and kicks...

"Gonna do what I should have done years ago, son!"

The blows make no difference, only staggering me. I've been through too much to care now, or feel pain. I rise, blood streaming into my eyes, blurring my vision.

Through the red I see his pointed face twisted into a sneer, spit dribbling down his chin, all but foaming. He has the little girl, the bar clutched around her throat. She's struggling. He's choking her.

"Have you met Heather?" he asks grinning. "She's your daughter, don't you know? Can you guess what I've been doing to her for the past few years?"

"Fuh... Fuh... Father ... Fuh..."

We turn at Juliana's muffled voice, all three of us. We're together in our shock at that moment. Together as we've never been before. She stands—barely—holding my gun outstretched in shaking fingers. Crying, she struggles to communicate, but words are slurred by drugs, or incoherence.

I feel like I should say: "Give me the gun," or something, but I don't know if she'd give it, and I don't really want it. I keep expecting the old man to say something, but he can only stand still, mouth wide, letting Heather escape from his arms like a small slippery fish. In the end, after our moments of indecision, there isn't time to say anything.

The blast roars. Everything else in the world has faded to silence. The old man is lifted from his crouching position and thrown back on the concrete path like a rag doll. When he lands, it's minus a large portion of his head.

Juliana stands over him, the gun dangling lifelessly at her side. She's trembling.

"Fuck you!" she says.

Lifeless eyes peer from that once pretty face as I bundle her and Heather into the car, and we drive away. I try to tell her who I am, but she can only stammer my name: "Joe? Joe?" The echo of a distant memory. Heather sits quietly in the back seat.

We head north, leaving the city limits far behind, taking the shortest route to the highway. I want to get away from here as soon as possible.

I'm a realist and I knew when I started this thing it would not end in a bed of roses.

As I drive along the darkening road, the rugged terrain blackens and closes in, leaving me wondering. How long we can keep going? I wonder if it's years or months or days we have together before we're finally torn apart and destroyed.

She is silent. I hope I will have a chance to talk to her again before the police catch up with us. That's all I ask. She's all I’ve thought about in ten years. Juliana. My sister. My first love and my last.

13

CAT PEOPLE

You can chase away the scavengers, the hyenas and vultures.

"A cat," Mwami, the local militia man smirks and picks up a piece of the body—a woman's forearm—gesturing to bite marks in the flesh.

You can sift and study what evidence remains of the animal that made the kill.

Anderson grimaces. He's used to death—but the bomb and bullet variety, not the tooth and claw kind. There's something more primeval about this type of death; ending your life as little more than *a satisfactory meal* for another animal.

You can't chase away the flies. Or the smell.

"What kind of cat?"

"A very big cat."

"Like the kind she's studying?"

Gabriela Karlsson had been a crypto-zoologist: specializing in the search for legendary or extinct animals.

"Perhaps."

Currently: she's carrion in the dirt of the African veldt.

"It ate her?"

"No, it killed her. The eating was mostly done by scavengers; you can tell by the teeth marks." The militia man tosses the appendage back among the pile of flesh and motions to his men to scoop the remains into a body bag. "You were her bodyguard?"

Anderson nods.

"Didn't do a very good job, did you?"

"She'd been warned not to go off by herself." Anderson picks up his XM8 assault rifle. Instinct and a general distrust of humanity has kept him alive while he's watched other more intelligent and more trusting men (and women) go to their deaths.

"It's also not a place for Americans," Mwami replies. "You'll be leaving soon?"

"I have to make arrangements for the body. Close up her camp. I don't intend to stay."

The militia man nods satisfied and returns to the truck with his men. Anderson watches them drive off. He's tired. His eyes dip to the crimson stained ground. A cacophony of noise. Restless animals call.

Sleep. Even if it wasn't for the sticky heat of the African night or the fear drenched sweat that awakens him, sleep wouldn't come easy tonight. First, his leg is still a problem. The mended fracture still brings pain; muscle and tissue lost five years earlier in a mortar attack in Afghanistan. Then there's the guilt he feels for her. Lastly, there's the damn cat. He can hear it stalking and crying in its compound. Does it know she's dead? It was almost Gabriela's pet. What should he do with the cat? Release it? Shoot it? The cat is calling. Anderson gets up and crosses the compound, avoiding the large wire cage on its perimeter, making his way to her tent.

Rummaging through her belongings he finds Gabriela's journal and flips it open at a random page, skimming the words and thoughts of a person now gone.

I hate and despise him. He is an animal.

It stings a bit to read the words. Not because it's a shock—he knew what she thought of him. He flicks back pages, mere weeks; her excitement and preparation for the trip, her journey from Europe, and their first meeting.

He reads:

I hate and despise him. He is an animal. I have never met a more loathsome man. If it wasn't for the university insisting on retaining the services of a... what do you call him? Bodyguard? Mercenary? His credentials seem in order: a decorated sergeant in the US Marines. He'd served in a series of hotspots. Afghanistan. Iraq. Was badly wounded during his last tour of duty and discharged, since then working as a security consultant in the world's most dangerous places.

I inadvertently insult him the first time we talk. It's the first week. We're out at the big cat compound. I try to explain the importance of my work while we feed the black panther.

"This one was shot and wounded near a township where it was bothering livestock. The locals get spooked sometimes. For years, there have been reports of a gigantic black cat, bigger than any black leopard, living in the mountains at high altitude. Locals have variously referred to it as the Jaguarete, or Black Tiger."

I show him photos of the feline thigh-bone that caused such a stir when it was discovered in this valley three years earlier. "The animal this bone came from is eleven feet long. It would make this one look like a kitten."

He studies the images with mild interest. "The species this bone belonged to could be long extinct."

"That's what we thought. So we radiocarbon dated it. It belongs to an animal not more than five years dead. If there are any others left, I aim to find them."

He nods and replies in his slow southern drawl. "And this one?"

"This one's a normal black panther. Actually, black panther isn't a separate species of cat. It refers to any, all—black felines that are large enough to count as a big cat. Science recognizes two types—one is the black color phase of the jaguar, the other like this one is the black leopard. We'll take it into the mountains and release it when it's fit enough."

"In the mountains you hope to find your mythical cat?"

"Maybe."

"The mountain and border areas still contain rebels. It's a dangerous place."

"That's why you're here."

"I'm just one man."

"Sergeant Anderson—how many people have you killed?"

"I don't really count."

"Women? Children?"

"Miss Karlsson—why are a bunch of cats worth getting yourself killed for?"

I meet his eye. "Sergeant—in the developed world the struggle to survive is no longer a great feat for humans, and therefore gene mutations offer little or no competitive edge. Natural selection is likewise a moot point; our ancestors faced significant difficulties, and many died before reaching adolescence, therefore those who were fitter and more likely to survive would pass their strong genes on to offspring. Without these two mechanisms working together, evolution for us, has all but stopped."

He raises an eyebrow and vaguely understands.

"Yet here's the prospect of finding a new distinct species that's evolved in isolation in a remote part of Africa. Where it all began. Life. Mankind. Everything."

"Not me. I didn't begin here. I didn't evolve from a damn ape."

"You don't believe in evolution?"

"No Miss Karlsson, I don't. I believe our Lord created us in his image. I'd have to see evidence to believe in evolution."

"Well there's evidence! Sergeant Anderson—you're not stupid. How can you not believe in science but believe in a supernatural deity?"

"Faith."

"Fairy tales," I stand and regard him in anger and confusion. "Goodnight Sergeant."

Admittedly it's not the best idea to make an enemy of someone who's supposed to be here to protect me. It's simply unnerving to still find educated people who believe in superstition rather than hard scientific evidence. I think I've always had this inquiring mind, this sense of not being satisfied with what I was told. I remember watching the family cat and wondering what made it purr. It's okay I didn't dissect Fluffy or anything!

He skips pages. Days flick by in a blur of paper and ink.

The first excursion into the mountains: we're assisted by local guides, used to tracking animals in the density of the jungle. The big cats are their forte. Humans are his. There are a few times we come upon burnt out camp fires. Or discarded Coke bottles. They're a reminder that rebels still operate out of this area. As a soldier, Anderson understands why. He tells me that the chances of government troops finding them would be remote. It's easy to blend, to lose yourself here. I know what he means.

He stays close to his charge. I know I'm difficult. He does his job and doesn't complain. I think in time, we develop mutual respect, and maybe more. A moment: I'm trudging through the undergrowth ahead of the others. He's having trouble keeping up. I know it's his leg injury. I don't slow my pace.

Suddenly, trees part violently, vines and lichens are ripped aside with ease as a mountain gorilla enters the clearing ahead of me. It's a silverback—a giant—a powerful, primal animal. Instinctively Anderson raises his gun, but I motion "no", kneel in the grass, and wave him to follow. Anderson obeys orders. The gorilla regards us cautiously; even to Anderson I suspect, all too human and comprehending. Satisfied, no threat exists, the silverback passes us by. I sigh with relief and turn to Anderson cheerily. "Smile. You just met your ancestor!"

He shrugs, brushing me off.

There are no signs of giant cats on the western face, and we descend to the camp.

"You're a violent man Sergeant Anderson." I know my harsh words catch him unusually off hand. We're drinking wine and more honest than we'd like to be. At least that's what I tell myself.

"I'm a killer," he replies candidly. "Would you expect less?"

"It's not your fault," I explain. "We are all in our way your ancestor's descendants. The most violent humans in our past, the strongest and most ruthless were those who survived to spread their genes. It's small wonder our world today is a violent place."

"You hate humans? That shows extreme self-loathing."

He's right. "Steven I don't mean to give you a hard time. We're just from very different backgrounds and believe very different things."

"I grew up in a small working class town. The kind Bruce Springsteen sings about. I could work in a steel mill or join the army. There were other choices. I can see that now, but at the time they weren't presented to me."

"I grew up in Stockholm..."

"Exactly."

I lean forward. Kissing him before I expect it. He's more surprised than I. I'm surprised when he returns it and it's softer than I thought it would be. I expected his lips to be hard, like granite. Our kisses are lukewarm at first, turning over to a fiery passion. I feel alone in the night.

I know I shouldn't have done it. Sex with him. I hate myself for it. I have more self-loathing than I can contend right now. So stupid. So instinctual. I'm not a teenager. I thought I was above that. Beyond that. It's dark now and I can't sleep with his scent still lingering tepidly upon my skin. I feel dirty. The cat is crying. I think she's well enough to be released. She deserves to run free with her mythical cousins.

I don't believe in them now. We've searched and found no trace. They're not there. The bone belonged to the last survivor of an extinct species. It's all a waste. I'm going for a walk in the jungle to think. I need to clear my thoughts, get the stink off me. My thoughts right now are those of a crazy person.

There's more. Anderson skims the rest, skipping the boring scientific bits from her last entry.

Gabriela walked into the jungle alone and died. Eaten up by it.

The cat's crying. He picks up his assault rifle, leaves her tent and trudges to the cage. Its eyes glinting gold in blackness; face to face with something animal and alien, with the beginning and the end, Anderson lifts the rifle to his shoulder and fires a single precise shot.

The camp's deserted, eerily vacant in the morning sun. The natives fled during the night; abandoning belongings and their last pay check. Tent flaps ripple in the wind, abandoned human nests. It makes life easier.

There's little else to be done. He visits the township before lunch and arranges the transit of Gabriela's remains to the capital, where she can be flown back to Europe. He returns to the camp, disassembling equipment, packing it away for transport.

One more night. At first when Anderson awakens, he's certain it's a dream. The kind you awaken, then reawaken from. You know the kind. The cat is crying. It's as chilling a sound as he's heard, piercing black in the night. An arthritic pain shoots down his leg as he stands, bringing him to a standstill. He pauses only a moment, reaching for his rifle, exits the tent and strides across the compound. The black panther carcass lies where he shot it, collecting flies and putrefying from the preceding hot African day.

But still the cat is crying. It's coming from the jungle. Anderson knows the man-eater is still out there. Gabriela's killer. The last loose end. His last duty. It would be sensible to wait for dawn and track it. Yet here it is. Crying in the night. Presenting itself. Anderson makes his way slowly into the undergrowth, treading softly as it progresses into dark jungle. It is near. It is big. Her giant cat? Her mythical cat?

As he walks, paper echoes of her last skimmed journal entry waft through time; crazy thoughts of a mad woman for whom time, everything has stopped.

There's an implication there. If evolution and the ability to improve the species has stopped for humans, evolution conceivably continues for other wild species. Could something out-evolve us? Could something else evolve from an existing species—as we did from apes—something that would in time become more intelligent and more complex and eventually replace us?

It's a crazy idea... unless...

In a tent the journal is dropping from his hands, unbelieving. He does not need science to explain the world to him, to give him a place in the universe or to give his life meaning. He has faith. He doesn't need to believe. In a dark and cold jungle at night he has his God, his gun and his faith. He doesn't believe.

Two days ago, Gabriela Karlsson is dying in this jungle. Something big is attacking her, dismembering her. With teeth and claw and precision. It takes her apart piece by piece like she was a jigsaw puzzle. Something to be removed and scattered. Yet it doesn't eat her. Most of the consumption is carried out later, by other jungle scavengers. Hyena. Vulture.

It removes her because she has become a threat and it is violent and strong and wants its place in the world. She's meek and let's be honest—will not inherit the world.

Whispers. Anderson recoils as he hears his name spoken in the darkness. A whirl of motion and pain. Red flecks dust the leaves of the nearby plants. He has lost his gun and his hand with it. He tries to run, but can only limp awkwardly, inferiorly. Tripping, collapsing, he turns and looks up. It stands over him, black, sleek, and shiny. It raises itself, standing majestically on two feet, its hands lethal claws dripping crimson. It's beautiful and clean and new.

Well unless... unless a species were to live in an isolated environment with natural selection acting upon it. Say a big cat. Then over generations it evolves slowly into something else. A kind of were-cat if you will. One that walks upright, and so has the use of hands, rudimentary tools and eventually develops or mimics a language. Then it could truly *rival man.*

Anderson feels its breath upon his face, hot and fetid, a drip of saliva as it opens its savage mouth, displaying rows of glistening razor teeth. He feels the touch of its claws raking slowly with precision across his abdomen. He hears its voice, low and guttural, as if gargling blood and understands.

He opens his eyes and believes.

14

YOU CAN SEE MY LOVE FROM SPACE

The past rushes over me in waves. I sit upon a rock watching a blue globe hang brightly in a black starless night. You should not live in the past, but for me, that's all there is. The future, in a moment, is cast to the winds. A small, insignificant particle in a storm of dust.

I meet Sandra at university. She is studying to be a doctor.

"I passed my final exam," she says, "and you?"

She knows the answer. Sandra always has her feet and future planted firmly on the Earth. Mine lie in the stars.

A cliché to think of all the westerners seeking themselves, but we honeymoon in India. In a rowboat in the Ganges, she reaches into the river and splashes me with ochre-tinged water.

"Looks like you need a blessing!" she cries.

In the city once named Bombay, I find something. In me. In her. Happiness. A completeness never imagined. *The Smiths* are chiming on the radio as we stand together on the hotel veranda and she turns to me, touching my arm. It's told in the Dhammapada that the Buddha said: *You too shall pass away.*

Knowing this, how can you quarrel? A glass of wine approaches my lips.

"I would be happy if I die by your side," she says.

It's a wish she will not realize.

I pick red-orange rocks, one after another. Man has a risky history of exploration. For every Columbus, there's a Scott. For every Apollo 11, a Challenger.

In training, I'm floating in a huge water tank navigating space station-like structures in the Neutral Buoyancy Facility at the Johnson Space Center in Houston, Texas. I am wondering how she will take it?

"It's down to just two crews," I explain. "One will be chosen, the other will watch on TV."

Sandra's face is turning away, unable to look at me.

Although there will be no TV. Just blackness and silence.

They cut communications eight hours ago.

Riding a roller coaster at a theme park; High-G is tugging at us. Sandra experiences a little of what I feel in space. The sense of weightlessness. Her hand clings to mine tightly. The world spins into blurred abstraction.

Holding arms, we share pink cotton-candy. I don't tell her then, but I know: my team has been chosen.

The storm is coming.

Dust storms are common on Mars. But not at this time of year. We're just unlucky. Collins and I are running for the lander as the dust cloud descends. A chunk of debris tears open his suit. I do not hear him scream.

Unlucky.

A black hole the size of a tennis ball crimps the side of the lander.

Unlucky.

When Sandra and I say goodbye, we don't know it's goodbye.

"I love you. I will always keep saying it, until I die," I promise.

"Please don't stop," Sandra replies.

Striding down a white corridor in spacesuit, sans helmet; I know Sandra stares forlornly at my back.

The President will, with a heavy heart, be facing the teleprompter and the nation about now. That's the plan. He will begin his speech.

"Fate has ordained that the men who went to Mars to explore in peace will stay to rest in peace," the President will say grimly. "For every human being who looks up at Mars in the nights to come will know that there is some corner of another world that is forever mankind."

And Sandra? What will she be doing? A NASA commander will be breaking the news to Sandra in a waiting room. She will hold her hand to her mouth. Another wife will be consoled in similar fashion. Dying is easiest for the one facing the end. For those left behind, there's only grief, pain and the horror of being left alone.

Beyond me is the planet Earth. Rocks of various sizes are scattered across the ground. I bend down to pick up a rock and examine it. There's no plan to bring me back, but I come upon a plan to live on.

I imagine Sandra dancing in a club. Lost in music, flashing lights and crowds of scantily dressed men and women. A surreal embrace of colored tones.

I must stay focused on my plan. On the rocks. My hands place one rock on a group of others already on the ground. They are slowly forming a straight line. And then another.

Mission control in lock-down. Staff hold hands over their faces, or are gently weeping. The plan: after recommendations on how to quickly end my life… "I'm sorry, Michael," the mission commander admits. "There's nothing we can do to bring you back. We must close down communication with the landing module. Everyone at mission control salutes you."

Abandoned into the void, a public ritual akin to burial at sea, the clergy commend my soul to the deepest of the depths.

I place another rock. Then another. My placements are meticulously creating a curve. At the limits of my remaining oxygen, I still have the time to complete my task.

Walking far from the lander, I look back at Earth and ponder exactly which moment I will rip the oxygen tube from the back of my spacesuit. I think of a future I will not know. Weeks will go by. Months perhaps, but it is certain that at some point Sandra will receive the phone call.

"Mrs. Sandra Jorgensen? I'm the director of the Herschel Space Observatory. NASA gave me your number. I'm not sure how to explain this…"

At first, she will not understand.

"We've found something we feel you should see. Yes, you need to come into our facility."

Sandra will stand in front of a huge space telescope. In trepidation, my wife will lean in towards the eyepiece.

The Martian surface as seen from the telescope will dissolve into view, barren, uninviting and red. In the sand will be a series of rocks arranged carefully in pattern. Will a smile crease her mouth? Will tears stain her eyes? Surely, she will understand, I did my best to keep my promise. Ad astra per aspera… in the sand… the rocks will spell out:

Sandra, I love you.
Sandra, I love you.
Sandra, I love you.

15

THE HEAVY METAL CAT

Allah's Apostle said... 'I have been made victorious with terror'
— The Hadith, Bukhari (52:220)

Cast iron molds stood by the open furnace as molten steel and copper poured down forming geo-metric shapes. The individual pieces, legs, torso, tail and head were cooled, taken out, polished and assembled into their final configuration. The Heavy Metal Cat was lovingly crafted by Arnold the village blacksmith as a gift for his young son Leo. All that remained was the brain.

Summers spent on the rooftop. Who wanted to leave the house wearing the mandatory heavy black clothing, and who would dare be caught outside without it? Here they could feel sun on their skin, the breeze upon unmasked faces and gaze across the skyline of the decaying city. As long as no one saw them in the street below they were safe. The rooftop allowed this pretense of freedom.

“It’s big,” Ivy said, always dreaming of escape. “I heard my parents once say that the world was not always this way.”

“I don’t know what to believe or hope for,” Pilar confessed.

“What could it have been like?” Ivy wondered.

“I daren’t ask.”

“They will make us marry someone. Our parents, or someone will come along and choose us a man, and we’ll have to marry them and be parted forever. That’s what happens. It happened to my sister.”

“We won’t be parted, okay? We’ll find a… way.”

Pilar inhaled the fresh air as pigeons cooed upon narrow ledges; car noise and gunfire the only noticeable human-made diversions. Then.

A name whispered over and over.

Omar Al-Nasawi.

Finally, Ivy asked: “Why do you still say that name, when you know he’s long dead?”

The window was closed, yet Pilar’s image refracted through it. As a child make-believe scenarios centered on favorite toys, the old dolls she assumed, belonged to her mother, or were scrounged from second-hand stores. Whatever happened to the children they once belonged to? That was a terrifying question in itself. Unimaginative people were spared quite a lot.

Two young children, a boy and girl, peered through the half-open metal rooftop door. Pilar said: “We have an audience—again.” With little encouragement, they popped through one after another.   “A story!” the smallest, the boy demanded. "The Heavy Metal Cat!" He sat and crossed his legs.

"Very well," Pilar agreed.

Her stories received a small audience, for very few children lived in the building; birth rates among the occupied being practically non-existent. Ivy was the first truly interested in Pilar's stories, often joining in, offering ideas of where a plot should go, or what the hero (most often heroine) should do next. Sometimes Pilar would accommodate such suggestions into her grand tapestry, though more than often, not. The first pubescent sexual fantasies which entered Pilar's mind, and triggered her first experience of masturbation, were of Ivy. At least some fantasies seemed possible then.

The boy's real cat Tomas had died the day before. Hit by a speeding vehicle, left lying in the road, body crumbled and squashed. Only the head remained intact. Arnold removed Tomas's brain, placing it in the cold metal cavity in the skull of the Heavy Metal Cat. He connected electric coils from the cat's ears to a battery terminal on his bench. Switching it on, the power surged and the Heavy Metal Cat came to life; screeching, groaning, his metallic limbs lifted him upright.

"What am I?" asked the Heavy Metal Cat.

"You are Tomas the cat," Arnold declared, "and you are back."

Blackened winter trees splintered down avenues enclosed by stark brick buildings crowned with brown slate roofs. A new mosque was being built on Catford Hill at the site of the old

King's Church. Scant construction took place these days. The damaged buildings remained broken, plaster falling off walls in crumpled sheets. Dangerous ruins home to squatters. Much of the general decay occurred after countless numbers of the occupied were evicted from exclusive residences, or simply taken away to camps.

Children played in the trash of the street. Collectors came sometimes, but there was too much to ever pick it all up. Everything ended up in the streets. Even the bodies. The headless, hand-less, corpses of the crucified on telegraph poles. Sometimes the bodies lay with the trash too long, till it was hard to tell if they were black, white, man or woman, adult or child. More trash that no one wanted to deal with.

No one cared anymore. Not the victors nor the vanquished. It seemed as if everyone was awaiting death. Not as something to be feared or really welcomed, but with the same resignation animals feel, upon detecting the first trace of blood on the path to slaughter.

"I do not like you anymore," Leo said. "You are too noisy. I hear you coming a mile away. You are too heavy to sit on my knee. You smell bad. You are ugly. I don't want to play anymore. I don't want you near me—go away!"

Tomas slunk off, tucking his tall metal tail between his legs. He desperately wanted his master back. Oh, he still loved him so. Leo was still sitting in the room, playing a computer game as Tomas watched. Electric eyes blinked in dark sockets. If tears could come, they would.

After, Ivy cried a little as they lay together. "What we are going through is a slow death," Ivy trembled. Ivy was Turkish; long black hair and deep brown eyes. Pilar: red hair, and pale beyond belief.

Pilar kissed her cheek softly. "Then we just have to stay alive a little longer."

"Why? Catherine killed herself last month. People are committing suicide all the time. We could, together?"

"No. At least not yet."

"What are you waiting for?" Ivy asked. "What is there to do? I can only cook and clean so much. I'm losing my mind."

Pilar felt herself drifting on the edge of sleep, but she could not sleep. Soon her father would be home. Ivy must not be found here. She needed to leave. They dressed quietly in darkness, hands lingering on each other's bodies, dragging out the final moment before Ivy's face was shrouded.

"I got your pills," Pilar called. No reply. Home in Putney. Beyond trips to the bathroom, Pilar's mother hadn't moved from the bed all month. Antidepressants made some difference in the past.

The bedroom itself seemed empty. Then, mild whimpering from the closet where the door was slightly ajar, and a foot protruded. Exchanged glances with Ivy; Pilar slid back the door.

Sitting on the floor amongst the shoes, her mother staring into space screamed in terror, hands defending, scratching, battling and biting at hallucinatory demons.

Pilar knelt down, took her mother in her arms and let the torrent take its course.

"Your pills. You know they will make you feel better."

Premature white hair concealing a much younger age, her mother's hands were shaking as she accepted the glass of water in one hand and medication in the other.

"Soon you will sleep."

Pilar stared at her own trembling hands while making tea in the kitchen. "Something bad happened to mother. Neither she nor father talk about it."

"If you want I can go," Ivy stood close to Pilar and touched her arm gently; skin tingling long after Ivy's hand had vanished, returned to her side. Fleetingly, a rare moment when everything felt good.

"I want you to stay."

Drinking tea in the living room with pretense of normalcy, Ivy giggled as she patted the cat. His furry body arched and pressed against her leg leaving white strands against her jeans. The cat who knew no better. A functional room with no decoration, no bookshelves, no books here, baring one. Not that either girl could read. An electrical splutter and the lights went out. The warm scent of kerosene wafted.

Love and life in Ivy; the coquettish smile, the taste of her soft lips. In her bedroom, Pilar took the doll off the bed and placed it carefully on the dresser. Locking the door, she pulled down the blinds. It had happened just like this many times before, yet Pilar could not quell the mixed emotions of excitement and fear. If discovered they would both face death, or worse.

Ivy's lips were the scent of lemon tea. Quickly undressing, they kissed softly. Ivy's long legs snaked against Pilar's body. Not here just for her own pleasure; her dear Ivy's pleasure was also what she sought. Ivy licked her bottom lip and smiled. A fire glowed in eyes of river-brown.

When Pilar handed him the water the young man drank thirstily, emptying the bottle.

"I can bring you more."

"No. It's enough for now."

"Let me help fix you."

The young man undid his jacket and lifted his shirt. "It's a bullet wound."

"I can see." Pilar padded the wound with the cloth and wrapped a long spiral of cotton around his chest. "You need medical attention."

"You can't help with that, but there's something you can do for me."

"Sure," she said. A good-looking young man, she realized, only a few years older than her. In another life he would be worried about finding a girlfriend. *Found her.*

"Firstly, don't tell anyone I'm here. I'm gonna wait for darkness, then try to slip through the patrols, but there's something else."

"What's that?"

"My name is Omar Al-Nasawi, and I am twenty-one years old. My parents are dead and I fear I will soon be with them."

"I'm sorry Omar. I'm Pilar."

"Remember my name. Will you do that for me Pilar? I believe as long as one person still remembers me, then I can't die, not really. Remember my name once in a while. Omar Al-Nasawi."

"I can do that, Omar Al-Nasawi. I can bring you more water too."

"Thank you."

Downstairs her parents hadn't moved. Pilar topped up the water bottle and returned to Omar. In the shade, they talked easily.

"Do you know much of what's out there?" she asked. "Is there a world beyond this?"

"It depends on what you mean by world. I grew up with fear and fighting," he admitted. "I don't know much else. I'm alive today because I hate the others a little more than I hate myself. Our battle has been a long one. Over the years, millions have died. I'm one of many."

"Don't be one," she said.

"I'll do my best," Omar forced a smile.

"You know things!"

"I know history. I've read a lot."

"You read too? Amazing."

"In Iran, we read. Books were very popular."

"What happened? I know almost nothing about… before."

"Ineffective, and indecisive leadership everywhere. While the West grew weak, an ideology masquerading as religion faced little dissent and grew in strength. Just as fascism was allowed to flourish without restraint in the 1930s. Few stood up against it or questioned what kind of world their children would inherit."

"You don't sound like a believer."

"Oh I am. A moderate, if you will. There are few of us left. But this is not a religion anymore, a cult convinced the end of days is coming and will do anything to hasten it."

"I want to help the resistance."

"You are by not turning me in."

She slipped forward into his embrace. At least in this purgatory she had all this, and he. A clock chimed somewhere far in the labyrinth. The afternoon call to prayer had begun.

Approaching dinner time, she departed to avoid suspicion of her absence.

A few hours later, as it grew dark Pilar returned to the rooftop. Omar was gone. Another dream, a story her mind created, except for the reality of blood drying in the corner.

Omar Al-Nasawi. Every summer she remembered.

Pilar's father passed in the hallway and nodded a cursory hello.

"How's your mother doing?" he asked.

Pilar shrugged. "Resting. She seemed… agitated when I came home. Was work okay?"

Semi-interested he slumped into the couch.

"I will make dinner. What would you like?"

"I don't mind," he murmured in monotone. "Whatever you care to cook is fine."

He switched on the TV. More good news about how well the forever war was going. After a while, he turned down the sound.

The scraping of potatoes in the kitchenette pervaded the room. After a while, she said: "It's not right, is it? This stuff they make us do and believe in. It's not right and it's not real."

A dead voice in darkness. "Do not say that ever again."

"But it's not—you know it isn't."

"If I ever hear you say that again I will beat you myself. There's no freedom to speak this way."

Pilar glanced down at what was left of the potato in her hand. It was gone. Everything was scraped away.

Leo no longer liked Tomas. His former friend sealed off in armor, all clanking gears and metal plates, had a smell of old oil about him and was no longer welcome in the boy's life. Pushed aside when he jumped on the boy's knee, Tomas the Heavy Metal Cat cowered on the floor.

"But it's me Leo. It's Tomas. Remember how we would play chase together? Remember how you would hide from me and I would find you? How you liked to stroke me and I would curl on your knee and purr? How you would tell me you loved me?"

Two bodies hung suspended, the lives that gave her existence extinguished; Pilar knelt at their feet in acceptance. Father had closed the store early, nothing out of the ordinary in that. Her parents had been together talking at the kitchen table mid-afternoon when she'd come downstairs for a drink. Their planned shared secret. Did they do it together, or did he hang her first then himself? Pilar heard no sound; it occurred sometime as the dark afternoon turned to evening. Why had they not included her? Answers she would never have.

Pilar cut down the bodies herself, laid them on the floor and called the funeral home. No questions followed, no need for authorities to be involved. The occupied were dropping like this each day. Progressive destruction of the soul, the funeral director intoned.

Pilar existed alone for a while; a ghost in an empty house with no one to talk to, nowhere to go… just the books which a stranger called Null provided, and the regular classes where he taught her to form words from letters in her own hand-writing, the basics of grammar, and began to extend her vocabulary. He never asked anything in return; then one day he did.

And it seemed so very little for the gift he had provided her.

She began to write and when she did, words spilled onto the page; ideas inside her too long neglected, required release. Null provided a forum: the fake *Dabiq* magazine; he published her articles, ideas, thoughts, and he went further, printing her subversive fiction as cheap chapbooks, scattered throughout the city, to be picked up and read in secret. He gave her an underground audience.

The little thing seemed so very small.

Pilar was determined to make the life given to her by dead parents count for something. Just what that could be, was for the time being beyond her. Pilar left the backpack in the overhead compartment and stepped out onto the tube platform. She thought of her parents' bodies hanging in the living room and all the irony involved in that.

Tomas the Heavy Metal Cat struggled to navigate the set of steps which led up to his home in the garden shed. He needed a lower gear. Gears whirled but wouldn't engage. Limping around the garden, alone and cold, it began to rain. Inside he could see Leo playing with the new puppy. Boy who was my life, will you not come and rescue me?

When Arnold the blacksmith arrived home Tomas was waiting.

"Hmmm... looks like your transmission has gone old fella," Arnold said after a cursory examination. "Gonna need to get you some new parts. It's gonna be expensive. You'll be okay to sleep outside a while? A tough metal cat doesn't need shelter, right?"

Tomas tried to speak, but his words came out as a silent murmur.

Listless, Pilar made her way up the spiraling staircase to the rooftop. Pulling on the metal handle, the door gave way into bright sunlight. She strode across the deck to one of the old chairs placed in the center. Light breeze touched her skin and ruffled her long black robe. A chill to the air. In one corner, a sound… subtle movement.

Spinning, fear came as she saw the man slumped in the shadows. a pistol pushed into the belt on his jeans. Not English. Arabian, maybe? No, something else.

"It's okay," he opened his eyes and held up his hand. Young, not far into his twenties, short black hair partially hidden by an olive-drab cap, there was something in his tone she could not place.

"Don't scream. I mean no harm."

“What are you doing here?” Pilar asked. “Who do you belong to?”

“Not *them,*” he said reassuringly. “I am with the others.”

Shia, she thought. No love lost between the two splinters of Islam. It was Shia the Sunni wanted Islam cleansed of most of all. Muslims would often be pulled aside in the street and questioned on their methods of practicing religion and prayer. Any hesitation or deviations from the Sunni way, and they faced summary execution. Death the penalty for apostasy. Death the penalty for theft. Death for pre-marital sex. Death for homosexuality. Death. Death. Death. One penalty for everything.

Still, uncertain, she edged to the door. “I’ll leave you then.”

“Wait! Don’t go,” he repositioned himself against the ledge, and she noticed blood leaching out of his T-shirt. He covered up with his jacket.

“You’ve been hurt.”

“Yeah. Can you please get me some water? Maybe something I can use to stop the bleeding?”

Pilar hesitated, and then nodded. She made her way back downstairs. A weekend; her parents were cold stone statues carved in chairs. She took a plastic bottle from the cupboard, filled it with water and passed behind them to the linen cupboard, taking out pieces of heavy cotton cloth.

A pitter-patter of rain on his metal back made Tomas look up at the grey sky. Rain slid down his face. He walked over to a woodpile in the corner of the yard. Rattling, Tomas began to shake. His bolts were loose, his cogs worn, his once shiny surface spattered with corrosion. He did not move all week. Although Tomas waited patiently, Arnold never returned. After a while Tomas the Heavy Metal Cat began to rust. Ferris-oxide scabs spread across his body, and he began to disintegrate.

Only inside his mind Tomas still lived.

16

GRAFFITILAND

Belladonna and Delaware walk into a bar. A little dive off Melrose, quiet for this time of the night. A television explodes with white noise. News about a political scandal in Washington. Palestinians lob a rocket into Israel. Belladonna leads the way to the counter, tilts her sunglasses down the bridge of her nose, and orders a whiskey for him and a *White Russian* for herself. They sit on stools at the far end of the bar. It's always good to keep a clear view of the door.

Delaware observes her tiny manicured fingers, wrapped like the legs of a spider around her glass, lifting the milk-drink to her lips. She's come a long way since he first met her. Never the type of girl he would have guessed himself ending up with. He'd met her in a church in Utah. It was during his directionless, questioning stage; he joined their church for all of ten minutes. Some days Belladonna used to say she'd like to go back to her Mormon folks and preach the word to them: the word of sex, drugs and rock n' roll.

She seldom speaks of those first seventeen years she spent with the cult. It makes him worry, especially when she hints at dark things in her past, and then retreats. He often wonders where she'd be if he hadn't saved her, converted her.

A middle-aged couple in a corner booth.

"They're both married, but not to each other," Delaware says.

"How can you tell that?" Belladonna asks.

"Because it's my work to know people. See the way he's looking at her, holding her hand, so gently. They're both very alert, on edge. Those two people don't know each other that well."

"You're full of shit," she says, like it's a surprise. Their eyes scan the bar. Two lesbians, sitting face to face. That's what Delaware likes about this place. It attracts a wide and varied clientele. One of the women is dark, with long hair, head bowed, and great glistening red in her lips.

"She's pretty," Belladonna says. "She's just my type."

The other?

"You can have her," Belladonna squeals.

"I like lesbians. I get along well with them," Delaware admits, raising his glass. "We have a lot in common. We both like chicks for a start."

"Why do you think the pretty dyke is going out with the ugly one though? I mean, couldn't she find a better looking woman?"

"I don't know. That girl must have something going for her. I always work on the assumption that lesbians have better taste than everyone else."

Who else is here? Few to warrant special attention. He enjoys these jaunts with Belladonna. It's like a hunt. He enjoys these moments of selection, of decision. He orders and drinks more.

"How about them?" Belladonna asks. She points to a well-dressed young professional couple. "They're just the sort who it'd be interesting to do it with—to wake their boring lives up. You can imagine it, can't you?"

He watches the woman. She's getting drunk, losing her inhibitions. The left strap on her dress has fallen across her shoulder, and she either hasn't noticed, or hasn't bothered to adjust it. From this distance he can see the outline of her nipples, pressed against sheer clothing.

Yeah, he can imagine. The man is oblivious to the woman's charms. He's very good-looking in a clean cut, unexciting way. He seems more interested in bragging to her, boring her, than taking advantage of her pliant state. He needs waking up. He needs to be shown the meaning of life. He needs to be shown what it is to really live. He needs Belladonna. Every man needs Belladonna.

The door. Shadows move and Delaware involuntarily slides his hand into his jacket pocket. Another customer. A man with dark, narrow eyes and a chiseled jawline. He wears a black vinyl jacket, and is scruffy, unshaven, long greying hair escaping from a blue bandana. He scans the room, twice, as if searching for someone, and certain, strides up to the bar and orders a drink. There's something familiar about him, but Delaware can't place it. It's funny, because he normally has such a good memory of faces *(scre—)*

The stranger looks down the bar, ostensibly to check out Belladonna.

"I know you?" Delaware asks.

The man's eyes flicker, red lines border blue pools.

"Doubt it," he grunts and slides along the bar, coming to a rest next to Belladonna. "Killing time. Do you mind if I sit here a while?"

Belladonna shakes her head. *Yes, or no?*

The barman brings a whiskey. A noticeable twitch in the man's hands. Something about the way he carries himself puts Delaware on edge. "You're a soldier?" Delaware asks. The man's skin has a rubbery luster.

"Was. There's some difference."

"Yeah, you're a soldier! I can always spot a man who's conducted violence in the name of his country."

"And you?" the soldier asks Delaware in a gravelly voice. "What have you done in the name of your country?"

"I don't have one," Delaware replies flatly. "But that's hardly stopped me."

The soldier nods understanding. "Have you ever heard about Harlow's psychological experiments on monkeys during the fifties and sixties? Infamous for their cruelty. Harry F. Harlow created the *Pit of Despair*, a dark metal box designed to isolate individuals from the outside world. Within days, the monkeys kept inside the pit were driven insane, incessantly rocking and clutching at themselves, tearing and biting their own skin and ripping out their hair. When finally removed from isolation, they were too traumatized to interact with others, and would become violent or suicidal when placed among their kind."

"That's horrible," Belladonna grimaces. "I love monkeys." *Hate people.*

"Dreams may inspire mankind's hopes for the future," Delaware says, "but it's only weapons, violence, and cruelty that make dreams reality. Scratch the scab of civilization, and all human beings are revealed as violent killers. A fake thin veneer resists reality seeping through."

"Mr. Soldier?" Belladonna asks, a nervous tremor to her voice. "Do you yourself have a theory of violence?"

The soldier thinks for a moment. His shakes dissipate and his hands becomes less agitated. You can tell he needed that drink. "Freud came to see us as the very worst of animals. Not gentle creatures who want to be loved, but those with an instinctual state of aggressiveness that shows itself in different ways."

"Like shooting mirrors?" Belladonna: smiling out of the corner of her mouth in that way of hers that's at once repellent and alluring.

The soldier bellows with laughter. "Shooting mirrors, why yes indeed. A noble pastime—and such symbolism!"

"Few old soldiers retire," Delaware says. "What're you involved in at the moment?"

Downing his drink and laying down notes on the bar, the soldier stares at his empty glass, his sad pale eyes multiplied in hexagonal crystal. "Y'know," he says, "that's true. We all have duties. Even if we sometimes go a little insane and lose track of what we should be doing." Belladonna's eyes rise to meet his. "Me? I'm not working on anything other than… I rather think I'm gonna go away and drink myself to death. How's that for a theory of violence?"

The soldier motions to a Christina Ricci-type blond who's appeared at the door.

"My date's arrived."

The young woman smiles seeing him, and he waves clumsily, a gesture Delaware doesn't quite catch. Leaving his seat, the soldier strides across the floor and exits the bar, blond in arm. A strange incident in a strange night. Belladonna squeezes his hand.

"Well, have you decided, darling?"

Delaware scans the room again. In the corner there's a party of eight or nine. Two families at first glance. A drink after a meal. All ages, but there's one girl—aged around thirteen or fourteen, sucking on a Coke. She's bored beyond belief. She would be fun. She would be very easy to draw away from the safety of the tribe.

He remembers the first time... Of course the first time wasn't the most enjoyable, he was nervous, and awkward. The first time was the hardest. After that it became so much easier. All he longed for was a partner. A partner in crime. Belladonna. It's so comforting to have someone with common interests. It makes him feel like he isn't alone. It makes him feel normal.

"Well?" she's becoming impatient.

He can feel the excitement rising inside. "All," he says, "or none? Wouldn't that be something?"

"What do you mean—none?"

"Because that's the ultimate display of control, isn't it? To know we have the power of life and death over every man, woman and child in this room. In a sense they're all dead now. If we walk out we're bringing them back to life."

"You're crazy."

"I'm God. With the power to take or give life." Delaware smirks, a strange cross between Elvis and Charles Manson. "Gotta piss." He gets up, walks across the floor, and pushes open the bathroom door at the rear of the bar.

Her boots click a little louder than she expected on the painted, cracked concrete floor. The scent guides her. He's hardly surprised when she pushes the door open; holding his penis in one hand, finishing, shaking the excess into the stained, encrusted stainless steel urinal. A smile washes across his face. "Baby," Delaware begins… waiting… and oh he shall receive.

Belladonna takes a knife from her belt, drives it deep between his rib cage and twists. The wet floor runs red. Soon it's he who's on his knees… stammering… questioning. He doesn't know why, and she's not going to tell him.

The soldier gestures two fingers to his temple.

Reaching out, Delaware grabs Belladonna's hand, so small and precious and warm. *(Faces screaming, random posters, these memories, this vision, something inside her has always wanted to squeeze life away with her bare hands. Maybe that's wrong?)*

After downing the remnants of her drink at the bar Belladonna makes for the exit. The two girls and the family have gone. Of those left, they look to her in a mind's eye, not like people, but one more distraction. Myriad computations. A moment's decision. A breath. She stops and locks the door.

17

CALENDAR GIRLS

"I'm a spy," Miloš confessed, allowing a sufficient dramatic pause before the punchline: "in the house of love."

Seated around a pub table strewn with pints of larger, none of his old tax ministry buddies seemed to grasp the literary allusion, nor were they obvious *Doors* fans, so rather disappointed he continued: "Or perhaps I should say, house of lust."

"Shouldn't you be looking forward to retirement?"

"Why take on something new?"

"How old are you now?"

Sixty-one.

"Go on, what's the new job?"

"I work for the council, undercover," he said, a semi-boastful tone to his voice. "I investigate illegal brothels. I bet you're wondering what that entails? Well, fucking mostly."

Silent blank faces stared, and then in chorus: "Lucky bastard."

Car lights glittered across rain soaked puddles. Miloš Novák walked wet cobblestone streets as darkness sunk like a heavy shroud over Prague. Fit, dapper in a grey three-piece plaid suit; hair in place, a whitening, trimmed beard, he stood out from slovenly, hunched contemporaries attired in cheap jeans and faded sweatshirts.

Down an alley off Ve Smečkách. Most of the growing number of illegal brothels operating in the city marketed themselves as therapeutic massage parlors—which made obtaining proof of sex work difficult. On a building pink neon flashed *Massage*, except there was a fault with the *M* so the sign flashed *assage* instead. A telling sign. Dilapidated wooden stairs led up a single flight to an entrance veiled with purple velvet curtains. Pushing through, a door opened to a bar where six scantily-clad women, long legs emergent from flimsy camisoles, sat on stools. The women appeared at first glance, mainly foreign—of Asian, Turkish or Arabian origin. Did they have work permits? How vulnerable were they to exploitation? Miloš shrugged. Hardly his concern. A lone customer lounged at the bar chatting to a surly barman.

Drink?

Miloš nodded: slivovitz, which he downed in a single shot. He felt the touch of a woman's hand upon his shoulder. Not an unwelcome sensation. Turkish girl. Her eyes, heavily made up, retained a hint of purity sinking in dark pool-pupils, and her nose was ever so aquiline, betraying her Mediterranean origins. Miloš found the girl immediately appealing. "Would you buy a lady a drink?" she smiled. "My name is Etugan, just like the Turkish goddess of fertility."

"Haha, well I hope you're not too damn fertile!" The other customer. He slapped her ass. "Wouldn't want a little whore-child looking me up in a few years!"

Could be some parlors offered just massage, although Miloš had yet to find one.

Etugan ordered a fancy cocktail which the barman made rather noticeably with water. The girls usually received kickbacks for drinks. Fair enough. Miloš turned to the man. Familiar. He'd seen him before. A regular. He looked him over in vague detail. Not exceptional. Miloš tried guessing his occupation, turning options over in his mind. Wearing a suit, sans tie could suggest businessman, office worker, possibly a retail manager. Hell, he could be a tax consultant.

"She's a good choice. Boobs a bit flat though," the man said. Etugan looked away awkwardly.

"Name's Štěpán."

Štěpán's handshake was clammy.

Etugan tugged at Miloš's arm. "Will you come upstairs with me?"

For a moment he'd forgotten he too was here to work.

Preliminary small talk reflected the nervousness of two strangers about to have sex. Etugan asked if he was surprised to find a Turkish girl doing such work? He shrugged, but inquired why she was, and she responded: "To pay for plastic surgery. Look at my boobs! That pig was right. I don't look good. My nose also. I don't like the hump."

"They are fine really," Miloš tried to reassure her. "Do you want to wipe away all trace of your ethnic identity?"

Etugan shook her head, yet appeared far from convinced. The topic closed and there was silence. “What would you like?” she asked, a stillness over her face. Her eyes could not meet his. He described it and she named a price.

Stripping herself naked, she took down his pants and began. Recording details in his mind for the subsequent report, Miloš found it difficult to fully enjoy the moment. He wondered about the girl. Was she in Europe legally? Possibly not. If that was the case she would be deported. He touched her dark hair lightly. Perhaps he should have chosen another. Still, it was all the same. The business would be closed and those involved charged. For the best. The people running these illegal joints deserved punishment. Details. Think of the details. She looked up a moment and smiled. He could not tell if it was genuine. Poor girl. He couldn’t concentrate. *You’re at work. Idiot. You need to finish it.* The courts definition of sex was quite specific: there must be satisfaction for one.

Twenty minutes later Miloš left, less than satisfied with himself.

“How have you been?”

Dominika seated herself at the wrought iron table. Her husband Janek nodded and slunk into a seat opposite. A quiet café, shaded from the harsh morning sun not far from the bustle of Staroměstské náměstí. They were thirty minutes late; Miloš took the time to finish the report for his latest job. Let it be said: most of the work was dreary paperwork. A wind gust picked a couple of sheets like dry brittle leaves. Quickly Miloš retrieved and returned them to a folder.

“Keeping busy Dad?”

She still called him that, even though he wasn't. Her real father had been killed in a car accident when she was still a child.

"A little. I'm doing a little freelance investigation." It somewhat made sense.

"Oh you just can't leave the tax world behind, can you?"

"An addiction?" Janek smirked. "How's the car? Getting it out of the garage?"

"The BMW's fine." Miloš always found the son-in-law stiff. Something decidedly off about him. A jealousy of Miloš's wealth permeated their interactions. Twenty years in senior positions in the ministry. Some opportune property investments in post-communism nineties, combined with a retirement package meant he didn't need to work. Janek, the plebe, the cog in the machine, hated it, and reviled his success. Something distinctly Czech in his character, common in many born in the communist era. There's an old Czech joke:

One day, Farmer Honza was looking sad. God saw him and came down and asked: "My son, why are you so sad?"

"It's my neighbor," Honza said. "He has a beautiful goat.'"

"Would you like a beautiful goat too, my son?" God asked.

"No. I want you to kill his goat."

Dominika laughed flatly. "I don't have much time," she said.

"Something came up at work. I have to leave in twenty. Where's the waitress?"

Miloš got up, went inside and ordered three coffees. When he returned she was talking on her phone. By the time she put it down the coffees were, even in the heat, getting cold.

"Sorry. Work," she shrugged.

"It's fine."

Miloš had intended his later years to be spent with wife of thirty years—Ivana, a plan which crumbled mere weeks after retirement. One evening he returned home to find the usually unflappable Ivana distraught with the news Vladislav, their friend and neighbor, had died suddenly. Placing his arm on her shoulder he reassured her that he too was shocked by the suddenness. "We have to be thankful we have each other," he concluded.

"Each other?" Ivana laughed. "Each other? I've been fucking Vladislav for the past five years. We were in love and I was going to leave you to be with him."

"You should give mother a call. She often asks about you. She knows you didn't want to talk much during the divorce but things change and people move on right?"

"Right."

"She's moved in with a guy in Ostrava. He's a doctor. No, dentist."

"How are your kids?" Miloš changed the subject. "It seems ages since I saw them."

"Well, they're busy too. Iva has just started her first year at Charles University, and Jan's in the last year of high school."

"I'll call in one weekend. I'll phone first."

Dominika downed her coffee. "Shit we're going to be late. We'll sit down again. Week after next?"

A part time job seemed a reasonable idea, and the advertisement intriguing: *Ideally from an investigations background. Must be single and willing to work nights*. The interview was relatively short. Miss Glum, the investigations coordinator flicked over his short CV.

"Have you partaken in the procurement of prostitutes in your private life, Mr, Novák? I know it's a difficult question, but relevant for the role you're applying for."

"Once or twice," he replied. "Before I was married." She gazed through heavy rimmed spectacles, probably sensing the lie, but let it pass, turning back to focus on his work history.

Reading the Prague Post on a train. It's almost a footnote on page three:

PRAGUE—Police do not suspect foul play in the death of a man whose body was discovered floating at the edge of the Vltava river Tuesday morning.

Police spokeswoman Eliška Klimentová said an autopsy is expected to be performed today. "We'll need to wait on the autopsy results to confirm the exact cause of death so it does remain under investigation until that time," she said.

An addiction. Perhaps Janek was correct? A bottle of wine consumed alone in his apartment and Miloš began to feel the temptation to cruise Prague's red light district. Fueled by alcohol, the night promised a hint of darkness and escape. His apartment was spread over two floors; on the top level a games and drinking room where he and his old friends played desítkový karambol. Plastered across the walls were explicit posters of beautiful women. He kneeled beneath one: a blue-eyed Czech blond, legs spread to reveal black panties, black stockings and garter belt, she leaned forward promising, but not quite revealing her breasts from a purple camisole.

A man entered the train and Miloš glanced up, regarding him for a few seconds: long, thinning, stringy hair, perhaps a few years older than himself. The man's two duffel bags were packed full and Miloš wondered where he was going? One bag opened slightly at the drawstring and he noticed it contained plastic. Plastic bottles to be precise. The man pulled the bag together again, as if ashamed, his forehead permanently wrinkled into a frown. He sat in a single seat, clinging to his belongings, a look of the terrified animal about him. This poor man, this fearful man, this pathetic man. His entire life was written right there in discarded plastic. He scuttled off at the next stop; Miloš sat watching him from the window until he vanished into urban wilderness.

Miloš exited the train onto Václavské náměstí at the Muzeum interchange. The street was awash with flesh; half-naked women in tight-fitting dresses, showing off long legs. In front of him the cheeks of a girl's ass threatened to burst from her shorts. Street hookers lined the square, hunting in shadows. A young gypsy-looking woman sprang forward and asked if he'd like a date? Miloš waved her away. Was this what they shook off the shackles of communism for? Grey Prague transformed into an orgy of tourists, bright lights and sex on display.

His destination: a glossy new club called *Calendar Girls.* No professional reason he should visit—the club had a license to legally operate. Inside, Štěpán was seated watching a topless stripper on the dancefloor slip slowly down a silver pole. He noticed Miloš, waved and offered to buy him a drink. Štěpán ran his own dry-cleaning business. The kind of guy Miloš could have easily encountered in the years at the ministry. He realized how inter-changeable men were.

"There's a new girl," Štěpán informed him. "Tuesday. You should try. Sexy, young body."

Here in the night club, the strip venue, the bordello, reality was laid bare—youth beckoned; the picture-perfect body opened to reveal its prodigious, tangible and timeless power. Miloš wound his way up a series of industrial iron stairs, reaching a landing with a central reception area, and to one side a series of cubicle doors. A look of emotionless porcelain, the flutter of atramentous eyelashes, a flash of vermilion lips, the glimpse of faultless flesh… ran creation. For a time. Emasculated, men threw money, wives, jobs, lives, into the abyss for a fleeting taste, for no more than a negligible instant. The receptionist took five thousand crowns for sixty minutes with Tuesday and pointed to the first door.

Tapping, then opening the door, Miloš found himself in a small room containing a bed, dresser and a silver pole. A girl began to move on the pole, lowering her bra strap; altogether sensual and alluring.

"Don't just stand there, come in," she ordered. She paused; piercing blue eyes slashed by eyeliner; black hair, high heels, mini-skirt and bra. A very young girl; she slunk back into darkness behind the bed as he approached. Nineteen perhaps? Hard to say with the make-up. He touched her arm, for comfort ostensibly, but accidently brushed her breast and found himself becoming aroused. She regarded him for a moment and her lips turned down at the corners. Her voice raised pitch. "I'm Iva," she said.

Off-guard a second, Miloš quickly recovered and sat with her.

"Miloš, what are you doing here?"

"I'm a spy," he accidentally stammered, then felt the need to conclude. "In the house of love."

"Anais Ninn. Sure, I'm such a big fan of hers," she smiled.

"You like books?"

"Of course. You don't remember? I guess you haven't been around in a long time. I just read this one. Take it—it's yours." Iva picked up a paperback from the dresser and handed it to him. "It's so rare to find people into books these days. I guess older people still appreciate them."

He placed the *A.B.C. Murders* by Agatha Christie in his coat pocket. "Thanks, no, I've not been around, and I'm sorry for that."

"It's okay. Here's another surprise. I'm a writer too. I write poetry. None of it is very good of course."

"Do you enjoy this job?" he asked

"Do you enjoy your job Mr, Novák?" the voice belonged to Miss Glum.

"I used to find it... okay," Iva replied. "I needed the money. I have done other things too. I was proud for a while, but now I'm less than sure."

"Well, I'm not sure if enjoy is the word I would use. Catching those breaking the law and exploiting others is always... useful work."

"What is it that you find… distasteful?"

"I was worried that you were beginning to like your job," Miss Glum responded. "Become one of them."

"I find men to be misogynist. The more I am around such men it disgusts me and makes me hate them and hate myself."

"Does your family know you're doing his?"

"I do not tell anyone."

"No, you're not going to tell them are you? Please don't."

"That's very good Mr. Novák. You're doing a good job."

"I won't. But why don't you ask your mother or father for money? Surely, they'd give it? You don't have to sell yourself this way…"

"Watch this memory unfold."

Mimicking normalcy, Iva sat with her mother and younger brother, Anton, in the living room watching TV as an open fire smoldered. Outside, arboreal movement in the family tree. Many branches. A chill permeated the air. So many leaves that melt.

"Please change the channel?" Iva asked her bother. "I'm bored with this."

Outside, a thump against the door, the echo of glass shattering. Leaves dropping, pitter, patter, onto soil. A key turned in the lock. Inside, Iva froze at the muffled curses of her father's voice. The door gave way and Janek tumbled in. He stumbled, standing at the cold throne of the living room threshold; a dismantled state, clothes disheveled, smelling of alcohol, a bruise circling one eye.

"Father—you've been drinking again. Fighting?" Iva asked.

"It's okay for you," Janek slurred. "For you! They treat me like I don't fit and I have to stand up to them."

"And it's nothing to do with you?"

Silence in an eternally reiterated masquerade.

"What?"

Dominika synthesized light shushing noises. "She didn't say anything. She's just a stupid teenager." A stand may blur the make-believe.

Iva wondered, as she had many times before, how Dominika had come to marry this man? A man? A protector? A provider? Then why this one? Did she, this ineffectual woman, view a glossy image in broad strokes without noticing the detail?

"It's fucking cold in here," Janek said. Detail: abuse.

"Can't you people even take care of a fire? Should I do everything?" Detail: narcissism.

"Where's the poker?"

No answer forthcoming, he knelt down by the fireplace. One log, fresh wood, untouched by flame, smoked. Reaching to flip it over, in his dazed state he instead grabbed the burning underside—and screamed, leaping back. Detail: alcoholism.

Iva giggled.

A silver thread of spit suspended on his lips as he slapped her face. Detail: violence.

Hands barely raised to protect herself, self-defensive wounds existed.

"Please, Janek, enough," Dominika moved between them, but even this reluctant motion was tainted by duplicity as she turned to Iva: "You shouldn't laugh at your father."

"I'm your father and deserve respect." Janek: a cacophony of details. "You're not the child I wanted. I'm glad I have a son."

"Why are you like this?" Iva cried. "Never mind, I'm going to my room."

"Not to play on the internet you're not," Janek not done, unplugged a wireless modem on a side table.

"I need it for my homework."

"You should have thought of that before you started this," Janek sneered, crimson faced. The forgery of domesticity toppled into the rhythmic tide of history. Men, more likely than women to perpetrate all types of violence, all of the time, almost; while the passive enablers who tolerate toxicity, sleep well at night.

"I hate you," she said. The decayed loam of this family tree, sluiced into drains.

"I hate you with a vengeance."

Miloš reached for Iva's hand, noticing for the first time, an arm covered in a lattice of regular cut marks. He thought of Iva and all the other damaged Ivas.

His spying activity took on a new dimension. She was correct that he'd had less to do with the family since the divorce. Ivana's grand-child. Not his. Feeling excluded from the family, he had let them drift. They had let him go too.

"I have done other things too. I was proud for a while, but now I'm less than sure."

It doesn't take a skilled investigator long to find her videos on Pornhub. He watched over and over again as two men ejaculated on Iva's face. She let sperm run from her lips and drip onto her breasts. One of the men spat in her mouth and she swallowed, dutifully smiling for the camera.

Outside, strangers' voices echoed in the courtyard.

Five am. Miloš waited near *Můstek* metro stop until Calendar Girls closed. On a lamp-post a sticker read: *I Love Porno.*

Iva left alone wearing a black faux-fur coat and took a train to the eastern suburbs. She got off at Strašnická and moments later Miloš emerged from the following carriage. Heels clicked on stone-surface stairs then rebounded to silence. On the street above she was waiting as he exited the station.

"Are you following me Miloš?" she asked.

It was futile to lie.

"That's a little creepy. Shall I ask why?"

"I've been thinking about you. I wanted to talk again. I can help you. I have money I can give you."

"I'm not your real grand-daughter. You aren't responsible. I have made my choice to be responsible, for myself. Do you understand?"

"I think so."

"If you want me to take your money, then you have to come and use me."

"I…"

"My mother always told me not to speak to strangers," she said. "I shouldn't have spoken to anyone. Not anyone ever. It's just I do not like them Miloš."

"Them?"

"Humans of course! Everywhere I go I try to be more positive, but I find it's the same. They are violent, rude and unpleasant. That's how they are. It's a myth and lie that there's anything beautiful or special about human life. We are all monsters! You aren't welcome in our family anymore, and you haven't noticed it?"

"I guess I know..."

"I've been having very bad thoughts lately. I have to stop doing this work because it's making me crazy angry."

"What kind of thoughts?"

"Well, just yesterday I put a knife in my bag before coming to work. Then I saw it and took it out again. Because I think if I brought it I would start stabbing the men there and I wouldn't be able to stop."

"You need to find another job."

"Yeah, I need to find another job. There's nothing good there. Only darkness. And death. The man they pulled out of the harbor this week…"

"I read about it."

"…he was a customer."

"You have to come and use me."

Miloš finally read the book Iva gave him. In it, the killer carried out a series of random killings placing their real intended victim somewhere in the middle to disguise the crime as part of a serial killing.

Calling her name, she appeared to him, opening the door to one of the booths. The lights were not on but he could make out sadness on the silhouette of her face and a wild faraway hazed look in her eyes. She slumped in the corner of the booth's couch, shaking. Miloš touched her hand and found wetness to it. "You've been crying?"

Her clothing seemed damp. Miloš leaned back against the door to let in some light and she lifted her legs to sit in a fetal position on the couch. The right side of her body was covered in blood.

"You're bleeding…"

"It's okay," Iva said. "It's not mine."

18

UGLY BEAUTIFUL

Sadness lingers around airports. Souls drifting in search of destinations. Returning to pick up the loose threads of a life… wanderer with a heavy heart separated from a loved one… to begin anew… young mother pushing a baby in a pram eager for her parents to meet their first grandchild… to return… to our terminus.

I finish my book. I buy airport snacks. As night settles I begin to question my sanity. I've always found airports gloomy places. Emotions probably experienced by everyone, and the paths we cross, likely the same. It's the territory of the ferryman, and who knows what heavy toll he may exact?

Don Mueang International Airport, Thailand. A myriad of voices, languages mingle as I exit customs into the terminal. It's 10pm and facing an eight-hour layover till my flight the following morning, and high airport hotel prices, I decide to stay up through the night. I've already been awake twenty hours including the thirteen-hour flight.

Sleepy… but naturally there's a Starbucks. Bangkok has one on almost every corner and the airport's no exception. Few comfy places to sit around the terminal, so I pace myself. A tall mocha should warrant lounging around for forty-five minutes to an hour before the staff might ask me to move on. I need to find a quiet place to myself too. I've a vlog to record.

Camera whirls.

"So today I'm gonna be doing the Q and A I promised you on Instagram. I got quite a few questions, so I'm not sure if I will answer them all, but I'll do my best. *ThrashNtrash* asks, if you could go back in time and discover the identity of the Zodiac Killer or Jack the Ripper, which one would you choose?"

"Well, Thrash, it's a tough choice, but I'd probably go for Jack the Ripper. On the condition that I'd also find out why. The motivation for the Zodiac Killer seems a bit clearer: in equal parts killing for the thrill and attention seeking. But the Victorian era, the London pea soup, the violent progression of the attacks, all make Jack more of a mystery. I'd want to know who Jack the Ripper was, and why—even if he was nobody."

Observation deck breeze tugs. Bright lights of a mega-city loom beyond as the sun sets. A young woman wistfully staring across tarmac. Dark skin, set off by short beige skirt and a pink Bob Charles shirt. Noting my presence, she turns, a sharpness across her face. An ankh, the Egyptian symbol of life drops on a cord around her neck.

"Sorry, if I'm interrupting your solitude," I mutter. "Just looking for a quiet place."

Her teeth flash ivory. "No problem, it's not mine. I'm leaving soon to catch a flight."

"Me too. Well in another seven or eight hours."

"Oh no. That's quite a wait. I just have an hour to go."

"Lucky you!"

She notes the camera. "You were going to record something? A video?"

"Yeah, how did you…"

"You're a YouTuber, right? I've seen some of your videos. *Cowboy & Tribe*."

"Yeah, you got it. That's me. It's nice to know someone's watching."

"What's the channel name mean?"

"Well, I guess… it just came to me, you know?"

"Yeah," she smiles again. "Jack. See I know all about you. My name's Rowena."

"You were looking pensive when I came up the steps, what's on your mind?"

"I looked unhappy? Well, perhaps. It's always disheartening when people let you down."

I lean on the rail with her, and she tells me her situation. Rowena Vermaak is from Kenya, but has lived most of her life in Australia, where she's heading. "So I was visiting my girlfriend's parents. I'm gay. Well, bisexual, I suppose. Occasionally I have slept with men. Oh, how humans like labels!"

Cut to bathroom, day. Rowena washes her face. As the tap water turns to a trickle she hears muffled voices in a distant room. Her girlfriend's mother's voice: "You've broken my heart."

"What are you talking about?" the girlfriend asks. "You said nothing before. I thought you'd realize I'd find someone I really care about one day."

"That's because it wasn't serious before," the mother says. "Now you're talking about moving in with this girl. You can't love her?"

"Thought you'd accepted I'm gay?" the girlfriend says.

"It's not because she's a lesbian," the mother finally admits. "It's because she's black. I don't want black people in our family."

Fade to airport, night. Rowena: "She didn't try to defend me. She should have told her mother where to go. Who takes their parent's side against their lover?"

I: "Well, the mother isn't worth worrying about. Nor, probably is the girl."

"Jack, you're white," she scolds. "You haven't had to deal with racism. I mean, I hate all that politically correct shit, but fuck, racism exists! It goes to the nth degree. Division upon division based on eternally shifting synthetic identity criteria. A Kenyan friend told me recently because I don't speak Swahili I'm not really African. So what am I then, I asked her? *Virtually white*, she replied."

"*Patti Kat* asks: do you intend to be a philosopher or a life coach? Not exactly. But I'd like to show people to live a life they want, not to live the way they've being told to live. Traveling's made me go in a different direction to the whole nine to five thing—do this, do that until you turn sixty-five or die. It may suit many people, but it's not for me. I want to do what I want to do firstly, and perhaps help others from there. Just because everyone else is doing something, doesn't make it right. If that makes any sense. Make your own goals and follow your dreams."

Barf. Would this be my answer if I wasn't pandering to an audience? I wonder who am I? Who is this *I* that can say who? And what becomes of the I, once the identity of the I trembles in secret? I was looking at a video of myself the other day and realized how much I am beginning to look like my mother. I can see her in my face. It's a strange feeling. I guess I'm now around the age she was when she gave birth to me.

I'm walking along Thanon Chang Khlan at dusk, carrying a copy of *Robinson Crusoe*—purchased from a side street bookseller, and contemplating what brought me here. A combination of rumination and the clang of metal-cage-stalls pushed into position by busy workers shoves me towards a beer at one of the street bars along Loi Kroh. The night bazaar is coming. I've been in Thailand only a day.

The waitress takes my order and leaves me alone with book and thoughts. What brings me here? Earlier in the year my father dies, a long relationship ends, and a short relationship ends before it begins, leading to in this order: a lonely Christmas, birthday and New Year, but this isn't entirely what brings me here.

Loss permeated my life the last years, and it absolutely contributes to my drinking, loss, and loneliness; it all comes from that.

"And you? Why are you in Thailand, Jack? Or is it a no-brainer?" Rowena asks. "A new video series, but I thought you'd have done South-East Asia by now?"

Sure, I have, and there is my escape. Instead, I tell the truth for once. "I'm here for plastic surgery. There's a little clinic in Chiang Mai—it's got great reviews—plus it's cheap."

"That's so strange," she replies. "You are not an ugly man. How old are you?"

Nor am I beautiful. "I'm thirty-eight. It's the age where anyone, man or woman can benefit from a little work. Perhaps, Rowena, you'll feel the same when you're my age?"

Rowena supposes, but she will not feel the same when she's my age. *Because you are beautiful,* I want to tell her. *You are perfect.*

"Who's to say what human beauty is?" she reflects. "It's all rather relative."

Unconnected and isolated, never capable of appreciating the raft of human malice thrown in each other's direction.

"Not at all. Human beauty is easily defined as the absence of flaws, rather than the presence of attractive features," I tell her. "This idea dates back to the Roman philosopher Cicero. Gods are the height of perfection; ugliness is then measured by how far humans depart from this god-like standard."

Not having an answer Rowena instead asks: "Can I watch you record your video? Then I'll be the first viewer."

I'm not used to having an audience, but I reply sure. She sits across from me while I talk to the camera and record. She watches, an eager, but silent observer.

"*Dazed and Confuzed* asks: so Jack, how did you start traveling? Well, how I started traveling… I visited a lot of places as a kid with my family. We'd go on these two week trips each year, usually to the north of New Zealand—the Bay of Islands or Coromandel. Then when I was in my late teens I wanted to go on some bigger adventures by myself. So I worked and saved up some money and went to South East Asia which is the best place to go traveling when you're first starting. It has everything for you, plus you can meet so many cool people. Then I travelled for two years throughout the UK. I started to work and then travel, and work and travel. And that can get pretty tiring, so I began to think about how can I can combine traveling and working into one. By then YouTube had come along. I'd always been into film-making but never really took the step of really getting into it. So it was like the perfect fit, from all angles. That's how I got into YouTube and traveling I guess."

Many hours awake and I feel disorientated. Outside, the terminal is cloaked in darkness, while inside, we travelers ghost-float through the concourse. A scruffy-faced German teenager sporting a *Deuter* backpack eager to return home. The dead or delayed littering the floor, buried beside their belongings. A first-timer frozen in a look of permanent confusion. I remember my first time stranded in an airport terminal. Christchurch. Snowed in. Gripping my mother's hand while my father goes in search of a taxi. About memory. About remembered and forgotten things.

"It was a good life, wasn't it?" my father asks as we reminisce in the hospice.

I nod. "It was." He did his best to make it so for those around him.

Memories are a deck of playing cards. Take out, shuffle, turn over favorite cards and there displayed is non-linear time. The playing cards are old and worn. I wonder if the purpose of life is to collect wonderful card-memories? The role of the present is then making sure possibilities exist for gathering. I wonder about my father, and why I can't be more like him?

Some shops do close.

I seek my third coffee, or is it my fifth? A cheap black number. I make it last. I go to the restroom. I am beginning to smell of BO and piss, and my hair looks like it hasn't been washed in a week.

"*Giacomo12* asks what's the number one thing you've learned traveling? Well, the more I travel the more interested I am in the world and the people in it. The more I learn that take aside culture, politics, religion—people are the same everywhere. They have the same wishes and desires. I'd tell people to not listen to what they hear or read, but to embrace diversity in every way."

Avoid Twitter outrage. China style censorship. Tow the party line. Read up on the Streisand effect.

"Do you ever miss your home and family; *Vanilla Sky* asks? Will you ever do a travel vlog about New Zealand?"

No, I will never go back to New Zealand. One of the dullest places on Earth. Small-minded people who are not very well travelled thus have a somewhat blinkered view of life. Charmless conversation unless you like talking about weather, rugby, how valuable their property is, or how nice New Zealand is. No culture, interest in science, books or art. They have nothing to talk about. They elevate fools to hero status. A low mentality populace who only worry about their status, with a low range of acceptable emotions. Women are equally unsophisticated and only care about looks, because that's all there is to distinguish the bland flock of males. Complex emotions can only be released through binge drinking. Stand out and you will be cut down to fit in with the herd. The major sport is hunting, fishing or finding other ways of murdering defenseless animals. It's no coincidence New Zealand has one of the highest suicide rates per capita in the world. Last year, over five hundred people took their own lives. I will never return.

If I wasn't a fake. If I had some sense of who I am, I would ask Rowena for her number or her email address, but instead I tell her to subscribe to my channel. She promises to.

"A last question: do I have any regrets in life?"

A pause momentarily—too long, and Rowena shuffles from her sitting spot, takes off her ankh and places it around my neck. I will wake up and all that was will be gone; there's only now. The moment. And in this moment surrounded by color and voices and a smiling Kenyan…

"Why do I have these dreams of perfection?" I ask, and she quickly replies. "Perhaps, because you need them... It's nothing to be ashamed of. It seems normal to me. Though I suppose if you knew about perfection beforehand, you might not ask for it."

DID YOU LIKE THIS BOOK?

Without reviews, indie books like this one are almost impossible to market. Without big advertising budgets; we rely on word of mouth and reviews.

Leaving a review will only take a minute—it doesn't have to be long or involved, just a sentence or two that tells people what you liked about the book, to help other readers know what they might like about it too.

The truth is, VERY few readers leave reviews. Please help by being the exception, and write a quick Amazon review. Alternatively, you could leave a review at Goodreads, or on a blog, or even just tell your friends.

You can leave an Amazon review here:
www.amazon.com/dp/9590800173

Thank you in advance.

SIGN UP FOR NEWSLETTER

Staying in touch with my readers is very important to me.

There are several ways we can communicate, including liking my Facebook page or following me on Twitter.

The benefit of signing up for my no-spam newsletter, is you'll receive exclusive free content, and you're guaranteed to never miss out on news, and new releases.

Newsletter sign up here:
www.shanefiler.com/subscribe

Printed in Poland
by Amazon Fulfillment
Poland Sp. z o.o., Wrocław

93611466R00117